SEVEN DAYS

OF THE WEAK

BY
DARREN THOMAS

SEVEN

DAYS

OF THE WEAK

Scream at the hollow
within the stars.
Shout at the distance
that separates beauty
from silent loss.
Run pain, gorgeous pain
an elusive twinkle of the night
Run home, run home.
We scream at the hollow
within the stars.

This book is dedicated
to the wisdom that dwells
within us all and to Jill.
She can be madness
but she is magic
there is no lie in her fire.

Part I

Prelude

The Long Wave Goodbye

A boy I once knew would cry.
He told me that he was beaten
with words spat from a raging mouth
on a Friday.
I could never understand his ramblings
but he would whisper that the world
always turned out a light that
dared to shine on his own dim thoughts
and imagination.
Sleeping with pirates
within another world
where their words never harmed
they hissed but soothed
and brought blankets
of ebony and silence
to lie still under.
That boy is now a man.
He told me that he no longer cries
for himself, just any man
that spits or ever spat
those raging words.

And Caroline will never know
just how her words would comfort
in a dark place.

1

The one-bedroom flat was just as he'd imagined. A kitchenette and follow-on living space set out in such a way that he already felt familiar with his new home. There was no 'one-ring cooker', instead there were four jet-hobs of a modern gas appliance on which to boil a kettle, a host of tinned foods, eggs and favourite soups. Another anomaly was that he'd always seen himself on a first floor. He was on the ground floor and the view from his back door was a clear view into a communal garden, contained within a standard wooden-fence boundary, the other side of which was a public area, where mature Ash trees were growing to such an extent that he couldn't help but notice that they would block out some of the 'south facing' sun.

He opened the back door and stepped out into the new garden. A designated space outside the full width of his most recent home stretching nine feet beyond. It was perfect. He lit a cigarette, inhaled a welcome hit of nicotine, before releasing a deep-rooted sigh that melded with the inevitable passive smoke.

As he gazed between the branches, he heard a birdsong. He was never familiar with what bird made what noise – but right now it added to the scene of tranquillity, and it was deserving of another hit of the cigarette.

'You'll be a sad, lonely old man!'

'Then I'll find myself a sad, lonely old woman'.

Smoking had a habit of evoking old memories.

Some words never leave you. The thing was, he knew she was right. He wasn't there yet. Sad or lonely. Though he'd been very close. He decided that 'Alone' and 'Lonely' were the same light-switch. It's a fine line between one and the other, especially when you're fumbling around in the dark, running a hand along a wall, and as you find the light-switch, the most you can hope for is being alone, it beats the dark of loneliness.

His mind returned to the birdsong, the trees, the pleasant sunshine leaning into his thankful face. It was a beautiful day.

He didn't have many personal belongings, so it didn't take him long to unpack. The Rucksack contained all his possessions, and most of them were clothes that he'd carried around a world. As he rummaged, he found the old Moleskin Journals that contained writings from over the past nine years, and THE Journal, the one from 1983. The one where it all started. He put that one straight into a draw, shuffling through the rest of them, reflecting on the days when he could afford to buy Moleskin Journals. One was a gift, he reminded himself. The one with the gold coloured tag into which was inscribed, 'Happy Travels – All my Love. Trouble. A- Ω xxx'. He smiled to himself. She was more than fuckin', 'Trouble'.

The Journals were full of musings, attempts at poetry, the odd piece of university work (death by morphology) and the odd mandatory doodle of a penis and balls. He kept them all because he'd decided that they were all worth keeping. It's not much to pass on to any next of kin – but it was all that he had left that could be carried around with minimal effort.

As he looked around the flat, he opened draws and cupboards to make sure they were empty, hoping there'd be a selection of fine foods in at least one of them. Nothing. However, underneath the kitchen sink was a washing-up liquid bottle that was half full. A near empty box of Daz washing powder, and a sponge whose 'spongy days' were well and truly over, baby.

Satisfied that everything was as you would expect, he returned to the back door and lit another cigarette. It wasn't as satisfying, it didn't need to be, but he savoured the nicotine anyway. As he exhaled, he began to smile to himself. A smile on the inside. It was the little things that made him realise he was making progress 'Progress – not perfection.' Not too long ago the washing up bottle would have been half empty.

He believed that he'd come through the worst. There was a long way to go, but overall, he believed things were on the up. The thing with 'belief' is that it can change. It's nothing more than the excitable children of contentment. As they grow, they change. He had some growing to do spiritually, but he'd dismissed just about everything that he'd once believed in. He'd weighed in every one of those beliefs and exchanged them for that one, 'no can lose', chip. That big fat chip of 'Faith'.
He sorted the remaining clothes from his Rucksack into two drawers, before deciding to go and have a walk outside. A first explore. A mooch. Find out just what was on the other side of those Ash trees? Hopefully, no one he would feel compelled to talk with.

He changed his footwear for a pair of walking boots. The ones that had been with him since Australia, that doomed trip that was a bold attempt to meet up with an estranged daughter, who it seemed had inherited the travelling gene and was herself scooting around a world with young verve and currently bouncing along Perth's coastline.
He never got to meet her, instead resigning himself to attend at an Open Mic event in Melbourne's Kildare district, a subsequent round trip of over 21,000 miles to read his poetry. An event that he attended but failed to perform. If he ever did write that book. That story would be in it.

With his boots laced and a sun shining, he was ready to face a world. He lit another cigarette. The first one of the day he didn't really need. Checking that he had his pen, paper and cigarette lighter, he walked into an unfamiliar brightness.

He still enjoyed writing and walking, they were the two things that he could afford. He couldn't afford cigarettes – but he smoked them anyway. He walked beyond the trees and followed the road before noticing a finger post stating, 'Canal 2 minutes', it was accompanied by a pictograph of a determined man walking with a head bowed.

Within two minutes he was at the canal bridge. On one side, the canal curved to the right and out of sight, on the other it was as straight as far as the eye could see.

He inhaled the last of his cigarette. 'Right, you sad, lonely old woman – where are you?' He paused for a second, before choosing to walk along the straight and narrow path. Even that decision made him smile.

2

That was the thing about Sunday. Too close to the rest of the
week. The old men walk the old dogs. Hangovers stand in small
queues. Twenty B n H blue. A disposable lighter. The sky
outside is Tupperware. A worker doing a foreigner. Today's
Football.

The amateur middleclass peloton. Cyclists are not drinkers.
Food served here. All Day Breakfast till 11 am. That still makes
him laugh. The list is endless.

There are no narrowboats along the canal. Liverpool is still 41
miles away. The seven ducks glide closer to the Mersey. The two
swans are undecided. A rare heron on the run. Hey, sexy legs.
Insects he doesn't know the name of. Flies. Midgeys. Being their
annoying best. They number the bridges the waterway people.
And the wide-beam in the distance. It belongs on the water of
Amsterdam. Blue and gilt. Majestic.

He greets the silent captain with a nod. An 'oreet'. Ignorant twot
barely nods back. That was the thing about Sunday.

You think too much. That's what the horses say to him.
Standing in that written about 'great green universe'. They're
even more beautiful in their rain and their silence. They know.
This path cuts away between the trees. There is always a way
through the wood. Knowing where and how to look. Take your

time. It's yours. You've earned this moment as much as that sunlight, breaking stubborn cloud with its being. Warming the nape of a neck. A welcoming like no other

Monday

His sight was fading. Like a father before him. Though that man declared that he had seen everything worth seeing. Another loss that didn't seem to bother the old man.

Everything?

There's only so much you can observe inside a newspaper. Two dimensional untruths that swayed him toward the left. The negative. Words are just turnstiles into the theatre of understanding. The game plays out. Win. Lose. Draw. The result is never relevant. The distraction is worth the investment. Fifty thousand souls. Heated arguments about a ball. At least he skipped *those* pages.

Maybe he had seen everything worth seeing after all?

Tuesday

We didn't know back then. We didn't understand. We weren't told we had to. Maybe because we didn't have to. Maybe they didn't want us to know what many didn't want to try to understand? There were lots of 'maybes' back then. And maybe lots of not really caring once you knew what they had to teach?

I've never used a book about logarithms since 1981. There're several in some distant landfill site. Long since eaten by the worms and those shelled insects that party under stones. They weren't ready for Pythagoras either. Probably choked on ratios or disregarded fractions as unworthy - food for thought.
The history of British railways was mildly informative. 'Stockton' and 'Darlington' were words he could spell but 'York' was his favourite - and 'Mallard' because it even sounded blue. Why was that?

Music with a bald sadist. The failed Tenor. We passed notes under the tables. Never in tune to the melody of understanding - but we laughed. That was our music. We would bang the drum. We were never beaten with anything more than sticks. Our skins were thicker back then.

We created art. We painted. We drew. We told stories when the paper was gone. The paper was always gone. She was a huge hippy. Jolly. Personable. Fine Arts degree. She smoked. We all smoked. There were 8 of us learning fine Art. None of us could draw. Or paint. Or sculpt. We could all talk. 8 too many for 'Sarah'. She never looked like a Sarah - but I guess that's Art, right there.

The library was quiet when it was empty. We read books for 35 minutes a week. Nothing learned. Nothing classic. Books about things easily forgotten. Religion and politics and a favourite encyclopaedia that spoke about vaginas. That was well thumbed.

The oldest man alive was our 'career advisor'. His handouts were small and made great paper darts. He said the culprits could work at British Aerospace - and he had a point. 'They

always need some idiot to sweep up'. He was funny.
He needed a sense of humour for at least 3 days a week.

Physical Education was for those that chose to run. Bounce
balls. Throw bent Javelins. There was a queue to throw bent
Javelins. THE bent Javelin. Footballs everywhere. Most of them
flat. Smokers everywhere - but just 3 cigarettes.

The girls were the school's saviour. Funny. Determined.
Resolute. Most were beautiful souls carrying the weight of
comprehension - but then along came god to spoil what would
have been a first party without balloons.

The first few days of the week had flown by. There wasn't much
in his flat, but there was access to the Internet. Not his own. He
was piggyback riding on a new neighbour's connection; a
generous man. One of those 'friend of a friend'. It wasn't
perfect but it was free - and it got him online. It also made him
realise just how thin the internal walls of the building were.

   He'd not spent much time surfin' the web. For a whole
host of reasons, but he realised just what an extraordinary tool it
was. There was no excuse for not doing anything. All you
needed was the motivation, some talent and an overall will to
succeed. Entrepreneur after Entrepreneur, Motivational
Speakers, Counsellors giving life advice, as well as 'Advice
Gurus'. It seems that all you need in today's modern world to
turn yourself into a success, is to tell your parents to 'Fuck Off'
and do your own thing. 'Parents, partners, negative people –
they hold you back, man'. Subscribe here. Click here. Like this.
Love that. It was the modern way – and do you know what? It
can work. It has worked, for some.

He'd been writing in his Journal about the walk along the canal, and through the nearby village. The working-class, lower middle class. That beige demographic of seasoned battery cells, too busy to know and too far down the rabbit hole to understand. He was that once. Digging away. Piling the wealth into the pockets of the one percent. Yeah, they drink their wine. Drive their financed cars. Spend at least a third of their day doing something they hate. Not all. Just the ones who think that they're better than you. They're the ones.

The reality is they're not all bad. They're just not as crazy as him. More conditioned to accept and deal with responsibility. More earthed. Just all round, 'more'.

Every time he goes back there in his head, he often goes via those memories of the old secondary school. He remembers those days fondly. They weren't all great. He enjoyed writing about them in his Journal. Such a shame it got burned down. He wrote about his father too. That was unusual.

Wednesday

Those days have long gone where he wore odd socks. Shoes on the wrong feet. An earring. John Player was never that special, but he did enough. Maybe too much. Time will always find a way to whisper what it must tell you.

The bruise of a pigeon. Though they're always 'cushy doos' since Glasgey circa 1987. It's standing motionless on an oak tree branch. Playfully being fanned by leaves. (Everyone should experience being playfully fanned by leaves. What a night that was). All enjoying themselves as the creator. Who wouldn't when you know what they know? He thinks 'Crann Bethadh, the Celtic tree of life.'

You don't need words beyond a certain point in the journey. Though you see them in life's rear-view mirror. Spilling from the back of a pick-up truck. You can afford to lose what you lose. You can let go of the wheel. Put your bare foot down on the metal. Feel the breath of the universe tickle your ears, your face, and each of the chins you've collected along the way. Ponder over Oxford commas. Nothing gets past him right now. He's on fire. A long way from planet earth. Just the element of no surprise remains. The universal paradox. He listens to the aeroplane. The bird. The motorcycle. The running water. It rained last night. There goes the glide of another train.

Thursday

Oscar did it. He would masturbate nouns. Ejaculate adjectives. It should have been a mess. Somehow it wasn't. I read what he did. How he did it. Sublime. After a while you could close your eyes. Read his words aloud. Things became harder. Underlying themes. Moral codes of ethics playfully wrapped in syntactic bows. There was enough room in his writing to squeeze yourself into. An old suit. Shiny, comfortable shoes. As if you'd dressed yourself for the first time as an adult. You saw the man at last.

Hank did it too. His words were dust. Fine pieces of Californian sand piled into heaps around a warm room. A home. I drank from those bottles he wrote about. The ones next to the one-ring cooker. The empty ones. The broken ones. The very few that never got touched. I fucked the women he fucked. I got fucked by the women that fucked him. He never gave in because he was never in. Always outside. That beautiful place. Hell, I can even feel the flies. I wonder what I must feel like to them. If I even feel like him?

And Billy. The man who could talk about the abstract. Like a priest would speak about god. Never really giving you an answer. Simply revealing the question that hides behind the words.

And the anonymous book about writing styles. Finding your voice. Don't always write in complete sentences. We don't often speak with standard grammar. Why should we write that way? Be. Creative. Be. You.

His new location was inspiring him to write. It's surprising what a few trees, the twitter of birds and unseen running water can create in a mind. He was getting all poetic and was unsure if that was a good thing or not? It's alright seeing things literally – but it's not often that he does. He wished that he did.

Even when he starts getting 'all poetic', it can be annoying. Talking in metaphors, analogies and allegorically – he feels like punching himself sometimes, so he understands how this can be confusing for others. Annoying, even. That was one of the reasons he didn't bother with people, and the few that he did, they were just as cracked as him.

That's why he started to read Bukowski. That man, he made sense of the world. He got it. As direct as the man's writing was, there is a deeper underlying message behind it all.

With all the upheaval of his recent move, he'd overlooked that the coming weekend was to be spent in Blackpool. A trip arranged so long ago that he felt that it was another person who'd agreed to go. He'd not been to Blackpool for years. The nearest he'd got was catching a local news bulletin talking about the town's demise and lack of investment. From memory the feature finished with a forlorn looking couple walking along a grey, wet and empty looking sea front. They were holding up an umbrella and walking with their heads bowed. It was a metaphor for 'despair'.

He sorted through his belongings; the most recent Journal was kept at his bedside. They all are whilst they are active. You never know when you may wake up in the middle of a night with a 'killer line'. You had to write it down. 'The faintest pen is more indelible than the greatest memory.' Something like that.

Friday

To be surrounded by madness is not always a bad thing.

'She is mad, but she is magic. There is no lie in her fire'. Is one that he recalls. 'Some people never go mad...what truly horrible lives they must lead', is another.

We each pass on the parcel of madness. Some take their time unwrapping its layers - others get straight in and tear at its worth. Wait until the music stops. And it will. In this game.

It takes character to hold hands with the crazies. Seeing self in other self. It's no wonder we're told we should fall in love. They're the crazy ones. The objects. They read their books. They watch their films. Write songs. Stare at the totality of nothing. Treating love like an ornament. One that sits in a window. In the sunshine. Dust free. Often behind the curtain.

Anxious of the adulation. Fearful of the black cat and the love of activity.

Saturday

I heard him telling someone that he loved spiders but had an irrational fear of flies. Yeah stupid init.

I turned slightly.
He rolled his left sleeve and revealed an arm inked in blacks and reds. Tribal nonsense. A clockface. And lots of spiders. Indelible madness from where I was sitting.

She seemed like a first date. She pointed to each of the spiders and was curious if they had names. Was there a web?

'You're in it', I thought. He just laughed and said 'no'. Then a poor joke about an elephant. How one fist was to stun. Another to knock 'em out. She didn't stop looking at him. The kind of person who swears down that a distant pylon is the tower.
'The next stop...is Preston'.
I sigh.
Then, I spot a fly.

This town could be an urban card trick. A residential sleight-of-hand designed to relieve a person of their hard-earned tickle. And in some cases - any fading will to exist. Today though its sea looks freshly polished. The lack of any fishing vessel another subtle indication that you ain't gonna catch much 'meat without feet' from any one of its three weary piers. There is no froth and bubbles at low tide. It seems the water is recovering too.

The joggers play their part. Speed walkers overtake those runners who puff their cheeks, check imaginary wristwatches. Introspection is what they seek.

You can stand in the shadow of a famed erection, in the shade of 19th century arches and marvel at the politeness of hammered in graffiti, 'Diane is lovely'. I don't doubt that for one minute.

The fortified concrete takes him to Gold beach in the 40's. Empty sands just before a legendary allied invasion. He can hear gunshots. Feel the madness of fighting for freedom. Albeit in another dimension. A seagull takes its turn to cry. Breaking another illusion.

The punks are here. A great palette of colour. Even greater hair. The best for midlife anarchy. Doc Martens. Seaside. He thinks of Martin Clunes. He can't help it. Port Isaac. Real sea. With fish, again 'meat without feet'. You gotta laugh.

Never Mind the Buddahs - here's the Hare Krisnahs. Flyers for spiritual enlightenment. In Blackpool. Fancy dress. Willy Wonka and an Oompah Lumpah. He baptises him as The Punkah Lumpah. Green hair. Orange face. He's quickly lost in the crowd. In this town. In this heat. In this.

He doesn't get to see his band. The Meninblackpool. Not tonight. Not here or wherever that place is right now. It felt like a circus that had performing animals. It was uncomfortable to watch. Outdated. Maybe that's all part of the illusion?

3

He looked back over what he'd been writing. It's always best to put it in a drawer and come back to it with a fresh pair of eyes. There were common themes. Madness, of course. Bukowski. Tick. Nature. Yup. A fine mesh of spirituality. Blackpool wasn't as cold or wet as he imagined it would be, though the train journeys were an experience worth writing about. School. His old secondary school from the 1970's. A school that survived two attempts to burn it down and several attempts to scorch its fabricated walls. Like its pupils, that school was a survivor – or it was until it was razed to the ground by the flame throwers of conservative economics in the mid 1980's. Gone. Brick by nostalgic brick.

He'd been writing like this for a while. At least since his most recent epiphany. The words were literally falling out of him. No sitting for hours at a typewriter and bleeding words from his wounds. No, these were falling. As if they were being channelled. They arrived already gift wrapped and ready to pass on into the ether. Gifting words to those who want to read. Alright, some of it doesn't make complete sense taken out of context, but maybe that's the key – they're not supposed to. These micro-fictitious pieces are channelled. Like telling a story in three words. It's possible. I. Loved. You. That's a story right there.

He was genuinely excited. His new surroundings may be helping. The meditations. Aid and assistance from a Higher Self. You're exactly where you're meant to be. He remembers those words distinctly and he felt an inner warmth as he repeated them. The warmth didn't last long. It rarely does. You're exactly where you're meant to be? The old cynic in him would say, yeah. Alone. Jobless. Skint.

However, he wasn't that old cynic anymore. He now knew who and what he was. So much so that he decided he was going to write about it. Rags to riches. Riches to rags. They're all doing it. It's fashionable to bare your soul. These celebrities are doing it all the time. Talentless celebs. If they've got a story - then he sure has. He's going to tell it. A story in the handcart of a journeyman. Even if it's just a tangible record of his existence. Even if it's only his children's children that read it. They may not want answers just yet, but they're afraid to ask the questions. That's all he did in life to get to this point. Asking THE one and only question worth asking. It was like winning a lottery. It only took him 52 years and cost him 2 wives, 3 children, several girlfriends, hundreds of thousands of pounds and, for a brief period, his sanity. Still, he was convinced it was all worth it. Sacrifice. It's a big word. See Jesus for details.

On the bare wall of his new flat's kitchen he'd pinned a calendar. He was bad with dates. His short-term memory was failing.

'12 Noon' was highlighted in red.

4

The room was small. It reminded him of an old Doctor's surgery from a distant past. The front space of an end terrace. Except there was no stale smell of cigarette smoke. No ashtray at the very corner of a desk, and no soft lilt of a deep Kilcorney voice to resonate and soothe.

It was more clinical now, no matter how they tried to round the edges. The Interviewer, much younger than the old Doc', appeared relaxed.

'What is your very first memory'? That was easy. He would often rummage through those images in his mind. So much so that past realities were often mixed with notions of another's memories, but he quickly sorted that jumble into piles until all that was left was a passing milk float.

He was standing in a garden facing a line of houses. All that separated them was a low picket fence and a road. Along that road passing right to left was a milk-float being driven by a faceless white coat. On the float were crates of bottled milk and a single crate of bottled orange. This crate was nearest the kerb right at the front. He remembers the sound of the bottles as they rattled nervously.

He was nearly two years old. Today was another day.

'I can't remember what I did yesterday. My memory isn't great'. The man facing him darted his eyes at a wristwatch.
'When was the last time you felt fear?'
'Today. Coming here'.
'Real fear. Have you *ever* felt it?'

'Have you?' he thought but replied with, 'of course'.

'When?'

He could give lots of examples but started with one where he suspected anyone would be fearful.

'When I was threatened by a deranged man carrying a large machete. He wanted to chop me up. He said it as if he would, but his eyes made me doubt him.'

'What happened?'

'I disarmed him'.

'How?'

'By using a weapon of my own'.

'Your truncheon?'

'My voice. I told him to stop being stupid and to put the weapon down. That way neither of us will get hurt. The language may have been less choice'.

'And?'

'And then he paused as he thought about it. He dropped the machete between us both. I told him to kick it to the side and he did. Then I arrested him. He was a big man. Drunk. Probably off his head but enough sense to see through the situation'.

'The situation?'

'The consequences. Even in Salford there's a consequence for chopping up uniformed police officers. Well, there was back then'.

'Was that one of the reasons you decided to leave the police?'

'Not that I was conscious of it. I thought I left because most of it was an illusion. A game. You see the game from a different perspective. You see the lies. You hear the lies. You have no choice but to acquiesce - or leave. Most choose to stay in it. Not because they want to but because they have to. The system's designed for us to become indebted. The deeper down that hole you go the more difficult it is to get out. If it was easy, they'd all be doing it'.

'Doing what?'

'Getting out. Leaving. Of course, there are some who love the job. They couldn't do anything else. They wouldn't want to do anything else. It's not a bad job. Some court the danger. I did when I was 30. I was fit enough to run away back then.'

'So why DID you leave the police?'

The question was a little out of context. That was the idea. He knew that tactic.

'There wasn't one reason. There were several. Sometimes the whole thing is greater than the sum of those parts. One man with a machete. Another with a gun. Bosses. Red tape. Politics.

They all add up. I'd seen enough domestics. Enough death. Enough bullshit. I didn't want to become one of those who moan and moan whilst they're at work. If you don't like it - leave. I was getting to the point where I wasn't liking it - so I left'.

'Any regrets about leaving?'

'course'.

'Such as?'

'I regret not leaving sooner'.

He watched as the interviewer turned a page in his notepad. He couldn't decipher any of the handwriting.

'Was there any time where you would considered yourself traumatised by events?'

'Well, I was forced to work at Maine Road on one occasion - '

They both saw the funny side of that, so much so that the interviewer wrote something down.

' - most days became a trauma. The pressure was intense back then, so god knows how they deal with it now? I've heard lots don't. They're leaving in their droves. Once the reality of policing hits you, that's when you must make that decision. It's not a job where you can only have one foot in the canoe. Get in or stay on the riverbank.'

'And the trauma convinced you to leave?'

'I guess it was other people's idea of trauma that finally persuaded me. People who complain about the police are usually the first to complain TO the police. About minor things. Things where it's hard to fake the sincerity needed to deal with'.

'Like?'

'Like 'my girlfriends sent me an abusive text message and I want her arrested', times that by ten times a day on top of everything else. It's no wonder heads go pop'.

'Did your head go pop?'

'No. Mine was more of a BOOM!'

The interviewer scribbled into his notebook. The longest scribble yet.

5

The old man was telling them about 'the hook'. Not just him.
There were other wasters too. Boys. Some paying attention.
Others digging the blade of a pencil sharpener into the previous
art of a wooden desk. Those desks had seen it all. If they were
men they would each be condemned men. No one cared of their
sustained abuse.

'Stop talking', the old man shouted as he chalked 'the hook' in a
scrawl. Blue scrawl. Into an A-board. Somebody had stolen the
white chalk. Borrowed it. Misplaced it. We all knew who except
the old man. He rubbed his blue fingers as the last of the chalk
disappeared into those seven letters. Turned back toward a wall
of indifference.

'The hook. Who can tell me anything about the hook?'
It was at that moment, from out that afternoon's air of
inattention, that he first began to see it. There it was. Hiding in
plain sight.

Monday

He arrived in Germany forty years too late. That was how long
it had been since the allies began sweeping up the devasting
mess instigated by a Third Reich.

RAF Laarbruch was nestled on the western side of Germany. It bordered with the Netherlands. In 1985 Germany was still divided with its Inner German Border **Innerdeutsche Grenze** and further still into Checkpoints Alpha, Bravo and Charlie. Berlin

was behind an 'Iron Curtain' and only accessed from the West via a complicated pile of officialdom. None of that was relevant to him in the West, *im Westen*. Cheap beer, cigarettes and petrol. That's all that mattered in the West. *Billiges Bier, Zigaretten und Benzin*

Royal Air Force life wasn't all beer and skittles. Sometimes it was just beer. In the autumn of 1985 life was different. Anything in 1985 prefixed with 'RAF Germany' said. 'Welcome to the 1950's.'

Laarbruch was as quintessentially English as any airfield back in the UK. The buildings were dated though the airfield runway was a respectable 2,565 metres long. It accommodated RAF Phantoms, Buccaneers, Jaguars and Tornados. As well as a whole host of visiting allied aircraft. It was Top Gun. Really Top Gun. And he was in it. The Danger Zone.

As he drove around the ring road, newly qualified with his RAF Germany Airfield Driving Permit (RAFGADP), he spent a moment in brief reflection. This time last year he was making Oil filters in some well-lit factory in the north of England. Right now, he was driving a left-hand drive (LHD) short-wheeled base (SWB) Landrover, carrying a BREN Light Machine Gun (LMG) with 300 rounds and two personal weapons. A Self-loading Rifle (SLR) with 60 rounds and a Browning 9mm pistol with a further 24 rounds (SLP). Life was ace (ACE).

The weak autumn sunshine was setting at the appropriate Zulu time. Two Tornado aircraft (AC) had just taken off and sprayed the beautiful scent of kerosene into a damp afternoon air.

Thud. What was that?

In his rear-view mirror, he could see something lying in the road. It was motionless but he didn't know just what it was? He pulled over. He contemplated activating his blue lights but decided against it. He didn't want to attract any unnecessary attention. Mindful to carry all his weaponry with him (don't leave a weapon unattended) he walked clumsily back to the anonymous shape.

It was a squirrel. A red squirrel - and as rare as they may be in Blighty, around parts of the Lowlands they're common place – or they were. At least one family lineage had ended abruptly.

As he was standing over it, the squirrel twitched. Was it dead? He poked it with the extended barrel of his SLR. It didn't move but he could still see life inside the sparkle of its eye. He was just about to poke it again; in the hope it may just be stunned (it didn't look squashed) before the light in its one visible eye faded. It was the first time that he'd witnessed death. He'd killed things before. Flies. Insects. Spiders but nothing as sentient as this.

He felt an overwhelming sense of sadness – a sense of loss.

He lightly pushed the squirrel from the tarmac with his foot, nudging it toward and onto a nearby grass verge.

As he climbed back into his vehicle, placing his weaponry down carefully, he had a thought. Two thoughts. Nothing profound. He was just thankful that the enemy behind that curtain weren't squirrels. And that whichever way he looked at it. He had his first kill. (K1)

Tuesday

They left them to die. To wither in the harsh suns of austerity and sobriety. Enough water to tempt the will of survival, another nail of the latest moon on which to hang the 'same old story'.

He sees it in the distant stars. How each of those will one day fade and leave nothing more than what they were before they started. Of course, we are born of stars and stars of us. They left us to never die. Simply to understand what it means to exist. What it means to become aware. And what it IS to live.

Wednesday

Those days have long gone where he wore odd socks. Shoes on the wrong feet. An earring. John Player was never that special, but he did enough. Maybe too much. Time will always find a way to whisper what it to must tell you.

The bruise of a pigeon. Though they're always 'cushy doos' since Glasgey circa 1987. It's standing motionless on an oak tree branch. Playfully being fanned by leaves. (Everyone should experience being playfully fanned by leaves. What a night that was). All enjoying themselves as the Creator. Who wouldn't when you know what they know? He thinks 'Crann Bethadh, the Celtic tree of life.'

You don't need words beyond a certain point in the journey. Though you see them in life's rear-view mirror. Spilling from the back of a pick-up truck. You can afford to lose what you lose. You can let go of the wheel. Put your bare foot down on the

24

metal. Feel the breath of the universe tickle your ears, your face, and each of the chins you've collected along the way. Ponder over Oxford commas. Nothing gets past him right now. He's on fire. A long way from planet earth. Just the element of no surprise remains. The universal paradox.

He listens to the aeroplane. The bird. The motorcycle. The running water. It rained last night.

There goes the glide of another train.

Thursday

He needed to drink more fluids. More water. Change his diet. Mix it up a little. Beef and Tomato Pot Noodles were as close to meat as he got. They doubled as ashtrays too, so he did his bit for what was left of the environment. He had started to think about death. Most people do when things start to fail. Start to ache. Start to pain. He wasn't afraid to die. He just didn't want to be around when it happened. To pass in his sleep would be a perfect solution. Though not great for any of his passengers. That made him chuckle. So did the word 'chuckle'. The world is a strange place. Sufferance on a Ball. Ain't that the case for the ninety-nine. Still, you've gotta laugh. You've gotta keep the art. It's all that separates us from another harsh reality.

He enjoyed reading back what he'd written about the RAF. It was inspired by a recent picture posted by an old colleague on social media. It seemed that everyone was looking much older. Though he couldn't make too much of the few days that followed. The usual torments about death he supposed. It was inevitable that he was writing about it. It was a constant theme

in his life, in his writing. Death. Loss. God. Love. Loss of love.
Stars. He writes the shit out of stars. Moons. The universe.
That's his favourite – death… by universe. Death by the breath
of the universe tickling your ears. Loser. Though 'sufferance on
a ball?'
He liked that one. He also enjoyed 'the hook'. He knew why it
was there. Obvious, really.

Cigarette. Bed.

Friday

On the odd few days he thought he was going to change the
world. On the even days he struggled to save himself. It wasn't
in him to save money, the whales or anything remotely
resembling a soul. If you're going to change the world start by
making your bed. He was paraphrasing some Doctor of
Philosophy, but he got the gist of what the doc was saying.
Some idiots took it literally. And that's just one of the reasons
why the world needed
saving. It was a big ask. More demanding than having to answer
a telephone, and he failed to do that on too many occasions.
If he was going to save a world, he would have to first decide -
which world he was going to save? The only ones he could think
of having any real chance of moving in a positive direction were
the ones he went to in his dreams. In his thoughts. They were
worlds too.
He made a decision. He was going to save the world that
bordered the madness. That world *really* needed saving.
And, it was right next door to a pub. Save a world. Beer.

Saturday

Experiment with style. Shorten your sentence. Lengthen where appropriate. Find your voice.
'There has to be juice in every line'. Yeah, that makes sense. It's not like bulling boots. Maybe it is? Think about it. Layer after layer. Nothing. Then boom. There's the shine.

Let them think that the dullness in layer after layer will be worth the effort. All they gotta do is read. All you gotta do as a writer is make them believe it's worth the effort. And there's nothing more exhausting than being compelled to read. And just when they think that all the meaning has been picked from the carcass of your words - make them want to suck on the bones of each following page, especially the last.

It was good advice. The sort of advice that could drive a man to drink. Write drunk. Edit sober. The best advice he'd read so far.

6

The previous week had started off positive, though the practicalities of life were often see-through and threadbare, he was at least beginning to write. If he was writing – he was safe.

Feeling into his jeans pocket, he produced 31p with 3 coins, a small key and a long expired 'All Day' bus ticket. The hum of the refrigerator was irritating his right ear and the chirping of an unseen bird was a melody in his left.

Last week's writing had started off well, reminiscing about his time in the Royal Air Force. He really did have fond memories of those times, but they'd become almost like a Babushka doll, images within images and they were soiled by the knowledge that some of the people who he'd shared those times with were either dead, dying, or on that fast track route to serious ill-health, and arguably, all promoted by a drinking that began way back then.

He concluded that at the end of the day, it was all freewill choice. One of only two things that exist in the universe. That and the Creator. He was conscious too that his writing was swaying with existential bend. Even now.

He had so many ideas about what to write, that they were slowly starting to pile into the sides of his head. He could feel the pressure building. He knew something of what to write; it was just the getting started. Like a Space Shuttle launch or a Saturn rocket. It's not Ok for it to leak out. It needs to be controlled. Disciplined. And right now, they're two words that seem only vaguely familiar.

7

The room still didn't smell of stale cigarette smoke. It seemed more clinical than he remembered, but it was something that he knew he had to keep on doing as part of the illusion. He was deep behind enemy lines. Back inside the Matrix. That's how he saw it.

The Interviewer was calm. He had a soft but high-level energy. If he was a cat, he would be purring with a voice just as smooth. 'Good afternoon. It is afternoon? Sit down'. He checked his watch to confirm before adding, 'Just…. How are things with you?'
'Ok'.
There was a pause as the man fiddled with an expensive looking pen. As if aware that I, that I, was judging him,
'A birthday present from my partner. So, tell me about your week. What have you been up to?'
'Well, I've been out of the house.'
'Excellent. Anywhere in particular.'
'The world of Blackpool.'
'Sounds exciting.'
'I went for the Punk festival. It got as excitable as Punk can get these days. It was good fun.
'Excellent. Have you written anything about it, anything in your Journal?'
'Yeah, yeah of course.'
'It still helps, writing things down?'
'Well, it gets things down.'

'Excellent.'

If he says 'excellent' one more time, I swear I will kill him.

'You're looking much better than when I last saw you. How're the practicalities of life working out for you?'

'The practicalities?'

'Yes. You were in between jobs the last time we spoke and living, as you described... 'sofa surfing?'

'Yeah, I'm not riding the DFS waves anymore. I've finally got somewhere to stay. It seems nice. Peaceful enough. No mad party people around, so the quiet life it is'.

The first scribble of the session with his expensive new pen. Then he looked back at me, expecting me to volunteer more information. Nothing.

'Did you speak with anyone at the Punk festival?'

'It was full of characters. Old and young alike. I didn't realise Punk was still a thing. Though I guess every Punk in the UK was there. It was good fun'.

I wasn't a great fan of phatic talk. Just cut to the chase, Charlie.

'Excellent'.

I swear to god I'll kill him.

'We finished off last time with you talking about some of your experiences within the police service. How 'harrowing' and 'traumatic' you described many of them. How you believe that as an empath, these experiences were exacerbated, can you follow on from that. You don't have to reflect on any particular case, just on the feelings you remember?'

Stupid question. He knows I'm going to attach to a particular memory. It's the fuel that's powers this train. I'll muddy the waters.

'Like I've said before, I don't believe that it was one particular thing. Not one sudden death, suicide or physical threat but a combination of them all. It's a cliché but there was nothing that I can say with any significance that stands out. I remember some more than others. Maybe you can tell me why that is? I'm sure it can be verbalised. Broken down'.

'The young man's suicide. You spoke about it in detail last time. The one involving an Immersion heater'.

'Yeah. Horrible. Both in its physical appearance and the obvious intent in the planning to follow it through. Heart-breaking'.

'You said you admired him?'

'Not at the time. On reflection. It takes some 'nads to plan your own execution'.

'Do you think that he would have been of sound mind to do what he did?'

This man is asking me what I think somebody else was thinking in the moments leading up to their own self-inflicted death? Dick.

'I had no idea what he was thinking, but I suspect I know what he wasn't thinking about?'

'And what was that?'

'He wasn't thinking about love'.

A second scribble with his expensive pen.

'Why would he not have been thinking about love?'

'None of us are getting out of this game alive, but there are better ways to get out than stringing yourself up in a cupboard after handcuffing your own hands together'.

'And how do you connect that to love?'

'Love of self. Love of god. Faith.'

'You mention 'self' 'god' and 'faith', how do you see each of those?'

'I don't see them as 'each'. I see them as whole'.

A third scribble with his expensive pen.

'So, to you, 'faith' 'god' and 'self' are one?'

'Absolutely'.

'So, by that logic. You are god?'

'I am faith. I also see self in other self'.

'What does that mean to you?'
'It means that as much as I may want to string myself up inside a cupboard on occasions. I choose not to'.
He looked down at his notepad but there was a slight pause before he quickly scribbled with what had now become the world's most expensive pen.
'Are you religious?'
'No'.
'How would you describe yourself in relation to religion?'
I paused. That kind of question needs considering, but I was guessing that was the idea. The pause was enough for him to alter his question slightly.
'What is religion to you. What does it mean to you?'
A dictionary's definition flashed into my mind's eye.

noun
a set of beliefs concerning the cause, nature, and purpose of the universe, especially when considered as the creation of a superhuman agency or agencies, usually involving devotional and ritual observances, and often containing a moral code governing the conduct of human affairs.

This was a long way from what I thought. I could distil it down into one word. The contrived definition left my conscious mind.
'Control'.
'Control?'
He was echoing my answers.
'Yeah. Control – and plenty of it'.
'Positive or negative control?'
It was a rhetorical question. I just raised my eyebrows, said nothing.
Another quick scribble of a world's greatest pen.
He hates me.
'Tell me more about your Journal'.

That was a little leftfield. What about the subject of religion?

'I write a Journal, have done for a long time'.

'How long?'

'Since around 1982. No. It was 1982. From the autumn of 82.
Dexy's Midnight Runners were number one. Eye of the Tiger.
Do You Really Want to Hurt Me?' It was all going on back then.
I was given a book diary for 1983 but started writing in it
sooner. Seven days per page. There were more lines to write in
for Saturdays and Sunday's. Monday to Friday you were only
afforded two lines. Probably one line for the start time of a shift
and one for the end. Even that seemed ridiculous. Contrived
somehow'.

'How?'

'It just did. Either way I started to document what I'd done on
those lines but not so much 'why' I did it? Though I do
remember writing down emotive thoughts for the first time. The
first time with any real conviction'.

'Do you still have the diary, the Journal?'

'I do – and I still read it'.

'What do you think when you read it. What do you feel?'

'It depends where I am in my head when I read it. Some days I
despair, other days I realise that it was those embryonic rustlings
in the infamous tortoise box'.

'Tortoise box?'

In my head I was singing 'Living in a box…living in a tortoise
box.' I blamed Dexy's for evoking deeply buried 80's cheese.

'Curiosity. Inquisitiveness. The first rustlings of becoming awake
to the world'.

He scribbled.

'And you still write now?'

'Yeah. I'm not preoccupied with who or what's going on in the
charts anymore, but I do write. Not all the time. Just when I feel
I need to.'

'When would that most likely be. Do you need to be in a particular head space to write?'

'Not really. Though I have worked out over the years that it can be cyclic, and cycles within cycles. Sometimes it just falls out and other times you have to sit and watch it bleed from you'.

'What do you write about? Anything in particular?'

'Everything. And nothing. That sounds crazy on its own, but that's pretty much how I feel where my writing is right now. Everything and nothing. Within nothing is where everything can and does reside'.

'I would like to read some. Will you write this following week and bring your writings in?'

'Yeah, why not?' I lied. I had no intention of showing him what he wanted to see.

'When you write your Journal, do you write it from the perspective of yourself – as the first person, or do you write it from a third person's perspective'.

That was an interesting question. I consciously write from a third person's perspective using past tense verbs. It is a Journal after all, – things that I've 'done' – not things that I'm doing.

'I often write from a third person's perspective'.

'Is, or was, that a conscious decision?'

Another good question.

'It was a conscious decision'.

'And why do you think that is?'

I had to think about that.

'Maybe to distance myself from myself…to allow the space for creativity. The ability to be the person I wanted to be, not the person I was…?'

'Are you protecting yourself from something when you write.'

Another good question.

'The truth'.

The interviewer scribbled. The final scribble was always the longest, especially with a world's most dangerous pen.

8

Sunday

You can't keep hiding inside your words. Tell them who you are.
Break through the shell of this life's madness. Stop talking
through the medium of 'He'. They see through that third person
anyway.

No. They see what they want to see. They're blinded by their
shortcomings, through no real fault of their own. That's their
responsibility. Their ability to respond. They're the thirds.
That's not who I am.
Who are you? He. You. I. Which?

Right at that moment, the voices had convinced him he was all
three.

Monday

He didn't see the city as Laurence saw it. One of them wasn't an
artist and one of them didn't work in the dark. The man's
paintings would've been less complicated if he did, save for 'The
Man on the Wall'. Maybe he did work the odd late shift after all?

This northern city was much less playful than those oiled stick
men, women and children that he alluded to. Times were
changing. Slowly. 'The Cripples' were still a part of its streets.
The anguish. The poverty. 'Going to Work' would be a near

blank canvas. 'Going to the Match' would have brighter yellow stick men with big hats and beards. And a first tout selling bendy tickets.

Its hospital is where he saw his first dead body. It's not unusual to see one in a Morgue. He'd seen lots on the tele. He was more than ready. Excited. Yes. Excited.

The building was isolated from the rest of the hospital. Mortuaries are discreet. Death is not the spectator sport it once was - or we *pretend* it isn't. However, the scent of the air changes in those buildings and never transfers from the celluloid of thrillers, horrors or any one of Lieutenant Columbo's fatalities. It smelt of death. Refrigerated death. Things were about to get a whole lot worse. He was still excited.

Since he was last interviewed he felt anxious. He hadn't felt that anxious for as long as he could remember, but he was conscious too that his memory wasn't what is was. Nothing is – is it?
He started to think about the paradigm of learning. How it's split into four. We start 'consciously incompetent' and as we learn more, we become 'consciously competent' – and as we become more aware, we're 'unconsciously competent'. We can do things without even being aware of our thinking. Like driving a car. However, the most dangerous place in which to be is the final quarter – 'unconsciously incompetent'. Where you're fucking up and you're not even aware that you're fucking up. This is a dangerous place to be. He questioned his recent decision making – was it born from 'unconsciously incompetent'?

He was writing about death again. He always went back to the
mortuary when he was thinking about death.
'You'll never see anything as bad as this'. Those words still
vibrate in his consciousness. They weren't true. He'd seen many
things worse than a controlled post-mortem. More sickening
than watching a lifeless body having the top of its head cut with
a circular saw and witnessing a brain being removed. Boiled eggs
had never been the same. Ironically, the post-mortem exercise in
'death experience' was the least bloodied version of dead bodies
that he would see. There isn't that much life in a week chilled
stiff – and the real shock of seeing a dead body 'for real' – a
freshly dead, comes with a demonstration of just how fine the
line from 'living' to 'deceased' is – that's where a first real shock
was rooted. Here one minute – gone the next. The reality of a
post-mortem is that they're clinical. Death is a serious business.
          He remembers the old quiz question. 'What's the nearest
city to Manchester?' To anyone south of Glossop, they would
cautiously answer with Leeds or Preston? It's Salford. That's the
nearest. Manchester's Siamese sibling. They hold each other's
hand. Whenever he thought about death. He thought about
'The Garden City'.

The more he dwelled on the notion of mortality, the more he
regressed to a childhood. He was thinking about death before
he'd even started thinking about existence. As a child he was
bombarded with phrases such as 'life after death'. 'The
resurrection from death'. Death was a common word for the
over moist ears of a child to absorb. 'When you die you go to
heaven' - unless you've really fucked up. In that case you go to
hell. There was even a stop-off place on the way down to the
ninth circle. Purgatory. No such autonomous place on the way

to heaven. Not that a seven-year-old boy could work out. He was still imagining the horrors of being burned alive in the sins of damnation. It was a lot to take in. Especially as his world was nothing more than the strangely coherent, 'Bap ba bap bah', of two Flowerpot Men, and the muted bouncing of a kid named, Andy Pandy. No one had the time to explain death to a seven-year-old. Everything was indestructible. Everyone lived forever.

Tuesday

Give me a child until he is 7 and I will show you the man.
He'd often run the Aristotle quote through his mind. Not least when he thought about religion. Maybe that's when it all started? The questions. Those open questions of 'who', 'when', 'where' or 'how'. The most searching question and perhaps the one that produces the fewest answers - 'why'?
Why is that?
'Who' or 'what' is god are small questions deserving of the biggest answers. WHY is god? Now there's one...

At seven years old, less than two years into a catholic schooling, he was indoctrinated into religion formally by making a First Holy Communion. He had little say in the matter. An indifferent Protestant father was challenged by a determined mother with the notion that Catholicism offered everlasting life. There were some drawbacks, as well as gaping holes in the logic of religion, but at 7 years old he was more concerned with not looking like a prat wearing a red tie, oversized shiny shoes and carefully coiffured hair. Big hair. It *was* the 1970's.

Catholicism appeared to be booming in 1974. A brand-new church was being built on or around 3 days of the week and even though the country was plunged into occasional darkness, the redemption of religion's light was there for all believers and infidels to see. Taking shape was a modern church next to a quintessentially English primary school, named after the Irish Patron Saint of Boatmen, Mariners, Travellers, Sailors and not least, Whales.

All of this passed by the boy who was more interested in 'Speed Buggy' cartoons, football and marbles. Religion to him was an inconvenience. An endurance of how much boredom a child could tolerate. Yet to some, especially the teachers, they took it very seriously. So much so that 'blasphemy' would not be tolerated. At seven years old he was a long way from being able to spell words with three syllables. He'd only just managed to write out 'God' and not 'Gob'.
And if you can know how to write 'God' at 7 - you will know how to right god as the man. Knowing is one thing. Understanding another, and just *maybe*, that's what Aristotle was talking about?

The school priest talked a lot about god. He was always in or around the school. He wasn't a quiet man. Neither was the headmaster. They would often be walking around the building together, telling boys and girls to 'hurry up'. 'Stop talking'. 'Don't run'. 'Slow down'. 'Get a move on'. Life was confusing enough.
As the new church was finally completed, another very important priest, more important than our, 'Slow down - get a move on' priest was to take the inaugural mass. As a seasoned school mass attendee, it was impossible not to sense the excitement in many of the adults' faces. This mentality was not the same for the children. He was only 7 years old. He didn't know anything.

He would stare at the blue sky. The night skies. The moon. The stars. Toward and into heaven. Further still into that murky world of not knowing. Not wanting to know. Jesus was another name. Another personality many spoke about. Jesus. He died on a cross. Jesus perished for us. Jesus forgave us. Jesus was born in a stable in Bethlehem. Jesus did miracles. And on Jesus's birthday, after a First Holy Communion, a Stretch Armstrong and a Raleigh Chopper magically appeared as an indirect result of Jesus.

For that reason alone he loved religion. And that other guy too. Father Christmas - who was much more real than Jesus, because he'd heard Father Christmas rummaging in his loft. Twice.

God. Jesus. Father Christmas. Life's characters started coming at him thick and fast. The one he was constantly told existed, he never saw. Heaven was a remarkable place just beyond the clouds and hell was a place zillions of miles below his size 5 feet. God? He was a guy with a flossy white beard. So too was Father Christmas. The resemblance hadn't escaped him. If you believe in one you must believe in the other. Though god was more persistent than Father Christmas. Once a year was nowhere near enough and god was way too much. They had their roles to play in his young life. He just hadn't worked out what that was? He was confused. Like the first time he'd tried to spell 'frankincense'.

As those early years were grinding away, religion slowly began to reveal itself. Catholics supported Glasgow Celtic. Protestants followed Glasgow Rangers with an equal enthusiasm. He hadn't worked out which of the two Manchester sides was what, or had even started on the two Liverpool teams, but at ten years old football was his religion and Alex Stepney was his only god.

His mother never went to church. She would pray at home to a whole host of saints, not least 'our blessed lady'. Though her instructions before sending him and an older sister to Sunday mass were precise. 'Make sure the priest sees you. Make sure you put THIS money into the offertory. Make sure you sing out loud and don't mime the hymns'. He had no intention of miming. He had no intention of attending mass.

Yet the older sibling's responsibility, especially as a sister, is to make a young boy's life insufferable with threats of 'I'll tell mum' and 'If you don't go, I can't go, and I want to go. I don't want to end up in hell'. Neither did he, but hell was just another word for 'church'. He'd already worked that one out.

'I don't need to go to some stinky mass' he suggested. 'Dad doesn't go. You don't go. I'm not going'.

'Tell him, Roy'.

'You're bloody going. Move!' His father's voice always got deeper when the authoritarian came out.

'Why can't I be a Protestant? They don't go to church!'

'Moooove!!!'

He sloped out the front door. As he looked back through a window, he saw his father exaggerating a mimed laughter before staring back into a newspaper, informing adults what was wrong in a world. What was right.

He went to church that day but still couldn't work out just how the priest turned wine into 'the blood of Christ' or, more importantly, why anyone would even want to?

Wednesday

The sound of the rain against the window was that morning's alarm. Like most people he found its melody comforting. God is in the rain. How many times had he repeated that mantra? The north was by that logic - very godly.

He enjoyed the north of England but the north west in particular. The sunsets were more natural. Watching a sunset from the east coast was like wearing gloves on the wrong hands. You could do it, but it just didn't feel right.

He was about to think about the notion of 'right' and 'wrong' but checked himself. Awareness.
The last few days had been filled with stillness. In stillness there is god. Quiet! Please. Be. Quiet.

Since an epiphany regarding his mother's death he had tried to dwell on its positives. His mother had died in the late winter of 2015. Nothing remarkable about the actual date until her death.

He was born 49 years 3 months and 10 days before she passed - or to put it into days 18,010 days. That's a lot of days. A lot of good nights out in there too, but the real intake of breath came a few seconds later when he realised the familiarity of those numbers. He was born on October 18th. How many times had he written 18/10?

The clues are always there. Yes, you can bend them to fit but that's life all over. We tolerate a size nine shoe with a size ten foot. It's all part of life's sufferance. We know it's not forever. Just until we get to that place, we call Home. Stop it. Stop it now.

That's the thing about awareness. You see things not just differently but even when that thing might not even be there.

However, if this book/novel is going to progress, I'm conscious I need to hold a reader's attention and I can do that in several ways. A sex scene. A new character - one less complicated and more affable. Someone you'll find yourself rooting for - or I can set up a conflict? Something that you'd feel compelled to read on. The long hard road to enlightenment. The nature of existence. The time I met Eric Cantona. Alex Higgins. Don Brennan from Coronation Street. Having tea and biscuits with the wife of The Chairman of the Labour Party. You're digressing again into the madness. No time for that. Clock's ticking.

Right, where was I... he?

Thursday

The room smelt of Linseed. So too did Mrs Jenkins, who wore the same tight-fitting red cardigan over a small selection of faded dresses during the course of her week. Each of which would've wrapped around the outside of the Royal Albert Hall.

If she wasn't teaching, she would've been protesting outside Greenham Common. She loved dogs and when she sat in the classroom 'marking', she would instinctively pick at the white hairs moulted from what you would imagine was a near hairless Labrador sleeping at home.
 'Can I go the toilet, Miss?'
"No, you can't, you've only got ten minutes'.
'Am bursting Miss'.
'Burst at break time. You've not got long as it is'.
'Miss, can I go?'
'Don't start John Linwood'.
'And me Miss'.

45

'Miss, who's that man over there?'
'Miss, have you got another pencil?'
'Miss, he's pinched me ruler!'
'Quiet!' No one is going to the toilet. The man over there is the school caretaker. No, I do not have a pencil. John give her back that ruler. Sit down. Be quiet. And Anne, start tidying that mess'.

Sarah Jenkins had a limit. All teachers did. Though her tolerance seemed shorter at certain times of the month. During those times she would often sneak into the storeroom, which conveniently had a skylight, and would light up herself a cigarette. Usually whilst the class of eight disaffected Catholics, nine including the teacher, scrawled intently on pieces of rationed paper whilst discussing the dilemmas of both Charlie's Angels and The Banana Splits.
'Miss, I can smell smoke.'
'Me too Miss.'
'And me. Miss? Miss? Miiiiss!?'
'Stop shouting'. She'd wipe her lips, partially satisfying her addiction as she reappeared from the storeroom sourcing PVA glue.
'Miss, can I go to the toilet? I really am bursting.'
'Just go, Daniel. Just go.'

As he left the room, Sarah Jenkins walked around the class looking over the shoulders of her now silent pupils. She appeared unimpressed with anyone's contribution toward a CSE in Arts and Craft. Where he had been sitting was a piece of A5 paper. She couldn't make out what he had drawn in B2 pencil until she faced the paper directly. It was an eye. Surrounded by laurels and shaded in such a way that it appeared to have some depth. To the side ran a series of fence posts with a fading perspective leading to a valley between two hills. The hills were clumsily drawn but the eye had remarkable detail.

The bell rang, signalling the end of the period and startling Sarah Jenkins in the process. The class jumped up before shooting out through a door, ignoring a weary order to 'keep quiet.'

Sarah Jenkins collected the drawing whilst picking up a rogue drawing pin from off an unused desk. She placed the drawing into her bottom draw before dropping the pin into a white mug, 'World's Best Teacher'. She checked her wristwatch before returning to the storeroom to finish the rest of her nipped cigarette.

The classroom began to smell less of linseed.

It was a Friday morning. He lit one of the two cigarettes he had left and noticed for the first time the picture on the near empty packet. A body lay on a mortuary table, covered with a white sheet. Maybe it had wormed its way into his sub-conscious and inspired him to write about mortuaries? 'A hundred percent of non-smokers die.' That thought alone negated any threat of an early death, and he enjoyed the day's first hit of nicotine.

There was nothing much more in his flat. No additional furniture. A box of 80 Tea bags – that was now 75, and three pictures, one of each of his children. He had 3 children. Often joking that he had one of each sex. He didn't really know what he was implying, either – but it often got some form of a laugh. He had 3 girls. They were now women.

Each of them was smiling at him. In one picture he was holding a daughter - they both looked happy. A father and his 6-year-old daughter. He looked young. He looked like a dad.

One day he was going to tell his story. Write that novel. He said that every time he looked at those pictures. At that picture. He was. He was going to tell his story. It was just hard right now. Some days he felt like he could write – other days he felt exhausted at the idea. He knew that he would have to resurrect past lives. Past emotions. Past ordeals and sometimes just the thought of this was overwhelming. He didn't have the space inside his head to create more fires. Sometimes you just gotta do it. Fight fire with fire. You gotta make it through those fires. He'd often associated fires with hell. Who wouldn't as a recovering catholic? (*too many 'fires' – consider revising)

He was going to write about it. Someday. Somehow. Right now, though, he was reflecting on what he'd been writing in his Journal. Where Mrs Jenkins had come from, he had no idea? A deep-rooted memory. Was he touching upon the significance of the 'Third eye'?

He was conscious too that his Journal entries were getting longer. More sophisticated. They were still written in that 'third person' slant, but they were beginning to make much more sense than they were a few months ago. The Interviewer had called it. Maybe he knew much more than he was letting on? He didn't really probe that far or too deep. The information was being freely spoken about. Earthed willingly from the roots of a personality. He was looking forward to speaking with him again. It was one of the few occasions where he could talk freely; in a non-judgemental way. Still, that's what the NHS was paying him to do. There were greater wastes of taxpayer's money.

He felt relaxed. Taking a long hit on his cigarette. As he gently blew out the passive smoke, he made a smoke ring. Then another. Their loose circles were pulled at by space and time, disappearing into the everything of nothing.

Friday

There was too much to say and so few remaining ways in which to say it. His thoughts had gone from queuing patiently, like well-heeled adults outside a Westend theatre to a baying mob of desperate souls scrambling for famine relief.

He had to think about that last description. Was it appropriate? You gotta give the truth.

Starvation was someone's truth somewhere. He left it in for now but knew it would end up on the long list of phrases that would gnaw away at him. I guess that's what truth does. Gnaws.
Try as he might he felt like he couldn't control his thoughts. A memory after memory was resurrecting itself. Skeletons of conflicts past. Growing from the rain of awareness like those relentless bones contesting Jason and his Argonauts. Here comes an animated night of infidelity. And another. Another. They're easily chopped down. Slain at the neck with deft blows of 'too young' and 'emotionally immature'. The spear of 'arrested development' through where their hearts once sat. Bring 'em on. Let them rise. He'll slay them all.

It had been a long time since he had dreamt about death. Longer still since he'd seen it, and what felt like a lifetime ago since he was paid to deal with it. Sudden Death.

He'd lost count of just how many and never made any personal notes to remind himself. He didn't think he would need to. The more noticeable ones never leave. Not the fine detail. Not the smell. Not even the colour of ink on that three worded note: 'Mam - I'm sorry'. Words have always been a killer.

Saturday

He was going to write a book. He is going to write a book. He was going to start today. At the weekend. The Journal entries are inspiring him. He'd seen enough. Enough of death. Enough of love. Hurt. Pain. Joy. He had all the relevant colours. He just needed to blend them in such a way that was interesting. Thoughtful. With enough of a word pallete to allow the observer to interpret what THEY see. After all, an artist's work is an interpretation of their soul and not their subjects. People needed to see and hear and read 'soul'. The best way to resonate soul is through the strings of truth. Play real. Play truth. Play soul.

He started writing down a list of 'Significant Emotional Events'. It'd been a long hard journey. He started with nothing and he still had most of it left. He wanted to describe his journey. He'd been on every square so far. That isn't an easy game - but it's the ONLY game.

1) Near death experience (x2)
2) Questioning existence.
3) First loves/kiss/sex/wives/girlfriends.
4) Relationship with parents/children.
5) Drink
6) Poetry
7) RAF
8) Police
9) Travelling
He was struggling. The list looked basic. It was his life after all.
10) Death
11) Awareness
12) Infinite Consciousness

13) Religion (affect)

14) Celebrities met (comic relief)
15) Journey toward enlightenment. Spiritual shat.
16) Suicides (affect)
17) Depression. Mental health. (Self and others)

He decided that he would write down twenty. The list was
sobering when he read it back. 'Pathetic' was another word that
Jet-skied across the lake of his mind.
18) Protagonist (Daniel Halland)
19) Irish heritage - time line?
20) Addiction.

That was enough. A vegetable soup of ideas. His broth of a life.
He questioned himself if he really had a story to tell? He could
create artistic license. A bank robbery? A murder? 'Too cliched'
he thought. If nothing else, he simply wanted to get down on
paper the fragments that had splintered from a mind. No point
trying to explain 'how' or "why' - people don't give two fucks.
They say they do - but in his experience - the vast majority
don't. You wanna find out who your friends are? Get yourself a
prison sentence - or depression.

He couldn't remember which came first, the chicken or the egg
of depression. The Black Dog. The Fog. The Gloom Lobster.

At least language made light of it. Just the thought of being
enveloped by the Gloom Lobster is enough to make anyone
want to burst into song. Just knowing that you can share your
days with a word processor and Geoff (he had a name for his
Gloom Lobster) can help creativity. So too does the threat of

boiling Geoff in the bubbling waters off the Isle of insanity.

He wasn't quite there yet - but he could see its coastline in the distance, and there'd already been enough in 2019 to make anyone feel 'Totes Pressed.'

9

He needed to sort things out. Things connected with his writing. That was just about everything. When he was writing he was peaceful. The madness couldn't compete with the words. Though without those words there would be no madness. He took a moment to bathe in the beauty of that paradox. The universe is a constant paradox. We all are. We are all the universe.

The idea of a novel had no real shape, it was still a slush pile of paper inside his head, but there were one or two good ideas. Some of those notions had come to him during his dreams, others as he would walk along the canal. There was poetry in and around that waterway. It just needed fishing out. Poems would write themselves. As the sun would rise and set onto the ribbon of its water, reflecting its patterns between the life of algae and the grip of its weeds. The swans and the ducks were always silent. Busying their days floating in late summer warmth. The signets would hiss at the curious dogs, but all-in-all their days were peaceful. Natural. Poetic. As natural as anything could be, sitting in the man-made waters of another thing separating Leeds with Liverpool.

He thought about his novel. He thought about writing poetry. Everything was looking, sounding and feeling poetic right now. Every story needs a beginning, a middle and an end. Though not necessarily in that order. And a good-sized book needs some significant words. In the best order. And a compelling story. That connects. Timelines. No holes. If there are holes, you can paper over them with the threat of another book. Label it Vol I. First in a trilogy. There are ways to dilute the mistakes. There are always opportunities to distract. Smoke and mirrors. Chaff and flares.

His mind was racing with fragile ideas. The last week's Journal had cultivated some deeply buried memories. Each of those was the beginning of a story itself. Yeah, so he went off on existential tangents. Hell-Oooo? That's what he does. He needed to step through each of them quietly, so as not to disturb their surroundings. Like you would be hunting for game. A different sort of tension on each side.

He thought about Jason and the Argonauts again. And his mother. And Mrs Jenkins. And Lowry. And dead bodies at the mortuary. And how they could fit into a story together. It was that time. He needed to mediate.

10

The room appeared larger than last time. Something had been moved. A bookshelf? A table? Something different. 'Hello. Good morning, good afternoon. It's always a fine line with a midday appointment'. The Interviewer seemed full of energy. Full of life. It was good to see.

'How are you this week?'

'I'm good, thanks'.

'Have you been writing much. Still keeping the Journal?'

Two quick fire questions, right there.

'Not as much as I would've liked. I get so far with a Journal and then I get distracted. I go off on one. Start writing…start writing bollocks, for the want of a better word'.

'Hmmm, what would you call bollocks, as you put it?'

'Exactly that. Like you said a while ago, just write down thoughts. No matter how small or seemingly insignificant they may seem. Well, I started to do that – then they quickly started to appear…small and insignificant, so I stopped writing them down. I was perhaps waiting for something a little more, a little more solid'.

'Did you bring anything in for me to see, for me to read at my leisure'.

'I didn't I'm afraid. I did intend to, and as we know, it's all about intent, but no. I didn't so much forget, I was just in such a rush to get here that I overlooked it. I have written some things though.

'Like?'

'All over the shop really. About the RAF. About an old schoolteacher. Even as far back as when I was seven years old. First Holy Communion and all that. I even wrote a bit to try and motivate me to write a book. It all seems to point back to the same place though. Back to asking questions about my existence. The meaning of life. The usual stuff'.

'Anything about your father? Your mother? Anything about any other significant loss?

'A little about my mother. I discovered that she died eighteen thousand and ten days after I was born. I was born on the eighteenth of October. The irony of any numerical symbology wasn't lost on me. It took over four years to see it but that's probably because I'm seeing more things, much more of the time'.

'That's good'.

'Is it?'

'Yes. It suggests that you're 'opening up' – as it were'.

'I guess so. I try not to think about that too much. I feel that I struggle sometimes with how much I've opened already. I need to consolidate that 'opening' and process that. I know a Journal helps but I've been keeping one for so long, I feel that it's become an extension of who or what I am. It doesn't assist in reinforcing 'why' I am'.

'It will – I can assure you of that. Just give it a little more time. You've made significant process'.

'Maybe. I feel like I've made some progress. Afterall, I'm not the same person I was – but who is?'

The Interviewer scribbled for the first time as he replied 'You'd be surprised. Ok, in the absence of any of your writing – I want you to listen to something. It's a guided meditation - '

'Hypnosis?'

'A guided meditation. It'll help. Maybe with your Journal, and with your thinking'.

'I'm not particularly comfortable with hypnosis, in any form - '

'Of course you are – you meditate don't you?'

'Yeah but - '

'That's a form of self-hypnosis. Relax. You won't think you're a chicken or a tea pot at the end of it.

'That's a shame. I need something to aspire toward.'

He smiled. He scribbled.

The rest of the afternoon was peaceful.

11

Whatever the hypnosis, the Interviewer, the meditation *did* – it did good. He remembers a softly spoken voice that had a familiar lilt, it sounded Australian, but he wasn't sure. It calmed his mind. Allowed any thinking to drain away through the gaps in his imagination. He knew he was peaceful. He knows when he gets to that state, he can envision cosmic and beautiful things not of this realm. A higher self. The actual source of Creation? Yeah, been there too. Without 'shrooms.
Some people would say he was crazy.

Sunday

To be surrounded by madness is not always a bad thing.

'She is mad, but she is magic. There is no lie in her fire'. Is one that he recalls. 'Some people never go mad...what truly horrible lives they must lead' is another.

We each pass on the parcel of madness. Some take their time unwrapping its layers - others get straight in and tear at its worth. Wait until the music stops. And it will. In this game. It takes character to hold hands with the crazies. Seeing self in other self. It's no wonder we're told we should fall in love. They're the crazy ones. The objects. They read their books. They watch their films. Write music. Stare at the totality of their limitations. Treating love like an ornament. One that sits in a window. In the sunshine. Dust free. Often behind the curtain. Anxious of the adulation.

Fearful of the black cat and the love of activity.

Monday

The day of his mother's funeral was a Monday. He was born on a Monday too. Little things. The weather was dry. The winter sun was there for display purposes only and offered no warmth. He remembers the backdrop to the entrance of the Crematorium. Green fields. Natural. The attendees were recognisable faces. Family. Friends. Ex partners. And for a brief time, all his children under the same roof at the same time. That thought only occurred to him much later.

The shock of those previous weeks hadn't been absorbed and it was a long way from being processed. Grief starts by numbing your senses. Like most of nature's stings. The numbness. The shock. The denial. The anger. The bargaining. The acceptance. There was a long way to go no matter what the self-help book may have said. Nothing prepares anyone for the reality of losing your biggest ally in the whole wide world. Nothing. And grief can cause a person to do extraordinary things.

Over the Rainbow was one of her favourites. Eva Cassidy's version. Somehow Judy Garland's original evoked images of flying baboons and wicked witches.
'I want Eva on my way into the Crematorium. Don't forget, Eva Cassidy's, 'Over the Rainbow'…and Susan Boyle as they send me through t'curtain. 'Wild Horses'. Don't forget…'

The image of her saying that days before she passed was all that he could think as he hoisted his dead mother's simple coffin onto a shoulder and began to walk in unison with 5 other male family members.

She loved a good funeral, and if she could have seen them all there as smart as pins and disguising their grief, she would have been proud. He had thought about this moment. Many times before. How he would deal with it. How it would affect him? Nothing he had thought came even close. He wrote a eulogy for her.

"First of all, may I take this opportunity, on behalf of my dad and my sister, to thank each one of you - family and friends - for attending today's service. I know it would've meant a lot to my mum to see just how supportive you all were during this sad and difficult time and for the messages of condolence and offers of assistance that were genuine, heartfelt and sincere.

Our mum had many roles in her life. As well as a mother she was a wife, a nan, a great-nan, a sister, an auntie and a friend – and with each role she tried to give it her all. She was an extra-ordinary woman who lived an ordinary life.

She often regaled tales about her own childhood. Which, like many just after the war, was one lacking in material worth but oozing with love both for and from her family. She lost her own biological father at the tender age of 6 months but was subsequently looked after by both her own mum and a man I would later get to know as grandad Bill. My mum loved Bill like her own dad – and later too her brothers and sisters Norah, Norman, Bill and Ellen. She always spoke wistfully and with great fondness of her relations back in a place she often described in magical terms – which in reality turned out to be St Helens – but like she always reminded me – it wasn't where you were brought up – it was how.

Her own childhood was filled with much love and happiness and mum attempted to perpetuate this love with a family of her own – cutting a mean buxom figure as a young lady, it was perhaps inevitable that she would date and marry at a relatively young age. On her 19th birthday she married my dad.

During the early part of her married life, both she and my dad were filled with a young love's sense of adventure. They travelled to Cornwall well before it was fashionable to do so – usually on 2 or 3 wheels, and lived a lifestyle that wasn't exuberant, but one filled with many of the little luxuries in life, like indoor toilets and running water. My mum always worked. Usually full time and nearly always in physically demanding jobs – often in factories. She spoke up until recently how much of her time spent working in those environments were some of the best times of her life – not because of the boring, repetitive work – but because of the people she met along the way, and how, on several occasions, some of those people became life-long friends, and many, I can see, are here today.

My mum loved all her friends dearly – but I'm sure she would want me to mention Sylvia, Maureen, Connie (from t'shop) and in particular Margaret (from Preston) – all of whom she would liken to being her sister.

I know how much she looked forward to spending time with Margaret every few weeks. Usually at Harvey's in Bolton for what was ridiculously known as a 'quiet' lunch.

On occasions, I picked them both up after these 'quiet' lunches and you would often hear them before you saw them – laughing and walking arm in arm like two schoolgirls. They kept each other young and their infectious laughter reminded me what a true friendship was all about.

These women may have been likened to sisters but my mum's surviving sister, Ellen, is more than deserving of a mention. Throughout the last few weeks Ellen has been a rock. She was there when my mum needed her to be and there when she was wanted. However, she had the ultimate responsibility of being the custodian of my mum's teeth – living with such a responsibility was beyond many of us – but Ellen once again shouldered that responsibility and so much more during my mum's last few days and beyond – and for that our immediate family is eternally grateful.

Families often drop into each other's lives at significant events – some happy – but some, like today, are often sad. The last few weeks were the most demanding weeks of my mum's life – who from finding out the true extent of her illness fought harder in one hour than many of us would in a lifetime. I always used to say that my mum was as hard as a dog's head. Her illness knows that now too.

It was a privilege to be with her as she passed away. Her sister Ellen, her brother Norman and my sister Chrissie were all there with her – each of them providing the lion's share of care, love and attentiveness to a woman they all truly loved – and my mum appeared to be aware of this – through her suffering she made us aware of her appreciation, often with just the slight squeeze of a hand. She died peacefully in her sleep at 9:15 on Sunday morning – perhaps appropriate that she died on the holy day, as she often berated herself for not attending church as often as she should, but she made amends with her faith by praying to a whole host of Saints at regular, consistent intervals. Our blessed lady being her favourite, and seemingly responsible for a whole host of miracles that occurred within the four walls of a family home over the years. I know my mum's unashamed faith and belief in her religion was rewarded for a final time as she lay peacefully in her bed, her face showing no outward sign of pain and it was obvious that she had found her peace.

There's a finality often associated with death and much of the sadness many of us are feeling now is often at the realisation that we'll never get to see or hear a loved one again – at least not in this lifetime. Moments like this can remind us of other loved ones who have passed on and even remind ourselves of our own mortality but it's important to also remind ourselves that death is as much a part of life as living itself. I know my mum wouldn't want her family and friends to dwell within the sadness for too long – while at the same time she would appreciate a humble legacy of not being forgotten – something that will never, ever happen.

My mum was a fighter. An optimist. A selfless, caring individual who loved others before herself. 'It won't always be dark at seven' was just one of her many sayings used to inspire, motivate and often boost any failing enthusiasm.

Her language could on occasion be described as 'colourful' and often it was my dad on the receiving end of her 'rainbows of critique'. She was an understated wordsmith. A comedian. A hardworking mum with opinions she was never reluctant to share – but beneath this veneer of steely righteousness was heaps of common sense, fairness and a true sense of what was right and what was wrong. What was divisive and what was encompassing. She loved every member of her family in equal measures and recognised and tolerated many of their shortcomings as much as she hoped they would recognise and tolerate those of her own. I know she died having not fulfilled some of her own humble ambitions. She never won the lottery - like she said she would. She never appeared on Who Wants to be a Millionaire – like we said she should. Instead she chose to encourage others to fulfil their own ambitions, supporting them in any way she could with the restrictions of overall long-term ill health.

Just before she went into hospital for what was to be the final time we sat and watched Mrs Brown's boys together. I'd not seen her laugh like she did then for a long, long time. I know she saw many of the traits of the character of Mrs Brown within herself. It would be hard to argue against it. My mum's entire life was dedicated to that of her family. A truly beautiful, selfless person. I'm not only proud to call her my mum – I'm proud to call her my friend and no words in any Eulogy will be enough to say just how much we will all miss you.
Good night Queen – and God bless."

It had been a long time since he wrote those words. The pain is still there. It never leaves. He just learned how to adapt to it. Something else most of us have in common.
Age is a great leveller. So too is illness. Unless you're both old and ill. His father was both. His mother often joked that her husband of fifty plus years wouldn't last two minutes without her. She was wrong. He lasted six months. So, before the end of the year he had lost both his parents. The last two people who had any real chance of fettering him to an institutionalised norm were gone. Taking their combined duality onto the astral plane

and more than likely still arguing the rights and wrongs into the beauty of infinity.

The symbology of a coffin going behind a curtain. Through the curtain. Through the veil. It's all there. All the world *is* a stage. We all get the opportunities to look through the curtain, to pierce the veil of illusion. Some don't wait until they're dead. Why would you? It's hidden in plain sight.

The Journal entry about his mother had surprised him. Significantly longer than anything he'd written for a while and the eulogy was practically, word-for-word. It wasn't the anniversary of her death, nowhere near, so he wondered why he was thinking about her?

What he hadn't mentioned was the amazing experience he had as she passed away. Holding her hand as she took her last breath.

Ninety minutes earlier he was talking with her. She seemed agitated when she heard any door of the hospital ward open and close. When he asked what was wrong, she replied 'I'm just seeing if the consultant was here. To see if there is anything, anything that they can do?' It was heart-breaking. Her body was ravaged with an illness that couldn't relent. It had gone too far.

You hear the professionals talking about 'end of life care'. It's exactly that. He looked at his mother. Exhausted. Pale. A hint of confusion inside the fading blue of her eyes.

'The consultants have told you where it's at. Your body is weary, and it can't fight this fight. Your soul is ready to soar, Queen. It's that time'. The words were the hardest words he'd ever had to say, but they appeared to be the words that she was searching for.
'You better have this then'.

She pulled the fine oxygen tubes from her nostrils and handed them to him, whilst taking what was to be a last look around the room. Seeing her daughter, her son and her brother with her. She closed her eyes. For ninety minutes she was breathing unaided. She became still as the agitation and anxiety slowly left her limbs and finally, at that moment, she passed. He felt an energy leave her and pass through him, carrying on into the ether. It was as if someone was pushing past him, and then pulling him from behind. She was gone. She was there.

Family deaths come in cycles. As each generation slips off the penny falls of mortality, you don't have to go too far back in a family history to convince yourself that the lineage quickly turns into nothing more than anonymous names. Writing about his mother's death had inspired him to look closer at the upturned stone.

One of his forefathers was called Daniel Wilson – his Great Grandfather. He knew nothing about him, other than a name. Another was called Daniel Murphy. A distant relative who, during the Irish potato famine of the mid-19th century, took it upon himself to head over to England in a bold attempt at survival. He made it as far as Liverpool before being nudged to the ninth circle of hell. Though in 1856 it was affectionately known as, St Helen's.

Death does create rustlings in the tortoise box of curiosity. He knew very little about his father's father and so he conducted some research. Afterall, if he was going to write a book, he was going to need inspiration from all angles. In a short space of time he had enough information to dampen the fire of curio.

Tuesday

'I remember my grandfather. He died in 1978. He was 85. His life's battlefields had taken him from the muddied banks of the river Somme in the autumn of 1916, through the relative calm of a Manchester's post Second World War numbness, before finally facing the demons that dwell within old age, ill health and memories gleaned from the former.

The story, passed down from the side of mouths of long gone family members , was that during the great war he was shot in the legs by a deranged German soldier, who'd slipped his fettered bounds, grabbed a handgun (never fully explained which idiot left a handgun lying about) and randomly shot at a small group of 2nd Battalion Seaforth Highlanders, who were simply enjoying the luxury of one of the few respites that bloody battles allow.

'Private Ernest Thomas' was the name etched on one of those 'dum-dum' bullets, which passed through both his legs and into the soft mud that enveloped everyone's sodden boots. That was the end of Private 3933's war and the beginning of an attrition which, sadly, wasn't unique.

At the end of the great war, he was awarded a trilogy of medals. including the 1914 Star (Mons), a not entirely worthless collection, but a pretty generic bunch of badges now worn on the right side of many a blazer. After the award each medal was placed into a tin box, together with his soiled Highlander cap, the usual letters of thanks from faceless '...in-Chiefs', these would be joined later in life by formal letters of rejection to requests for financial assistance from the relevant post war(s) departments.

Like many men of that era - my grandfather never spoke about the war. All the proverbial war stories came third hand, often embellished (at least i hope so) and told with an underlying respect for ANYONE who had lived through such savage horrors both at home and abroad. Of course, we must remember THEM. ALL of them. The men, the women, the children and just about anyone who had to live through such a dire existence - often with the ignorance to comprehend the political and economic persuasions at those times. Each of them would be fighting their own battles for many, many years to come. Often influencing their offspring as they did so - but the one thing that got most of those Brits through the adversity - a sense of humour had to prevail.

Ernie Thomas moved from the monochrome of an inner-city Manchester and toward a slither of colour that dwelled within a town inside a bowl. The cotton mills of Bolton were no easy place to work - but after the horrors of 2 wars - a production line dominated by women was manageable. During the rest of his hard-working existence 'Dad', as he was affectionately known to anyone, continued to work, relying more on his brain than on his legs (for obvious reasons) often citing his own philosophies about life.
'Semi-skilled?' Tha's either skilled or tha's not.'
'Put thee money in there son, you'll soon save it up.' Pointing my father in the direction of a newly installed coin gas meter.

My own father visited 'Dad' most weeks. Toward the end of 'Dad's' life he would sit in his infamous armchair, hidden behind a plume of blue sweet smelling pipe tobacco, his fingers a deep mustard colour, hands riddled with a 'nuisance' I later found out was cancer - which he often cut out of those hands himself with a favourite pen-knife. (they really were a different breed) as he listened to the wireless that both glowed and heated a small part of the space where he sat.

One day during a visit, my grandfather gifted my own dad a box. It contained his Seaforth Highlander cap and the rest of any post war correspondence. I got to wear that cap. Surprisingly it fit my fat head - even looking a little small, and in the excitement of seeing these rarely spoken about items, my father took a picture of me wearing it. It exists somewhere. Both the hat and the photo. Somewhere.
Not long after, the illness did what the 'deranged German' didn't.

With a translated motto of 'Aid the King' the Seaforth Highlanders have melded into a singular Scottish regiment along with many others. Money once again being the ultimate reason. Remembering those men (and women) of distinction. Of courage. Of bravery.

Of course, we will remember them. How can we EVER forget?

Wednesday

If there was more to the man, then it never fully revealed itself - not through his son. Not so a young grandson could see, but he wasn't always going to be that young grandson. Not always going to view a world literally. The experience of life gives you a different set of binoculars through which to view a world. You feel it differently, and with that shift in awareness comes 'truth'.

Thursday

The moment had arrived. His truth had finally washed into him. Yeah, it had taken its time, but few men remain young men for too long. You have to be ready to harvest the crop. Nature's cycles. Evolution of mind. Untie the knots.

It takes more time than many imagine. They collect their crystals like the sand gathers its seas. They talk and words cascade like falling rocks. They become less not more. Less of the earth they'd hope, but they weigh the same with or without their words. A bird stops becoming what it really IS the moment you think it's a bird.

The clever people solve the riddles. The wise avoid the question with questions that lead to the one and only answer.

He'd watched some of it being born. Some of it passing. He felt it more when they did. A duality. THE essence of what it truly is. There are NO words to describe it. None exist than can take its weight or cast it out.

Don't let religion fool you. And it will. As long as you allow it. The smoke and mirrors of those who know. They keep it for themselves, but they hide it in plain sight. They have to. That's the game within the illusion. We have each and every key but there's only the one lock worth opening. One that can only truly be opened to its fullest extent. That door. That is THE way.

Friday

He couldn't fly an aeroplane. Not back then. When the days were tage and the nights were nächte. The real Airmen played Tom Jones to scare away the birds. The irony.
The men over there could fix things. They wore a fourth propeller and always looked like they did nothing. He had to walk. Run. Carry little metal jackets and two weapons. Open barriers, gates and doors but was always told to keep a mind closed beyond a certain point.

There were hundreds of keys. The same amount of locks.
Blisters don't just develop on feet.
Saluting the Crown. Pilot. Flying. Flight. Squadron. Wing. Station. Don't rise above your two 'V"s. Have a bit of THAT, Sarge.

He saw through it. All of it. The puppet masters. The Ministry. The illusion of establishment. The concrete shapes loaded onto Charlie One Thirties. You could see it all from a tower in the clouds. But the beer taste good. And the fritten. So that's where he learned how to drink. How to swing a club. Bowl a ball. Hold an Epee. Recover. Drink. Repeat.

He preferred the dark. When the Rodneys were night-time flying. Eating the fumes from kerosene. Exercising under falling snow. The odd clear sky. Standing amongst the rabbits, the red squirrels and the moles. The theatre for a colder war. Daylight from orange sodium's. The distant stars of afterburn. One day he will write about this. Without giving away any of its secrets. Through adversity to the bars.

Saturday

He had the honour of knowing some beautiful people. Truly
creative beings who could paint and write or play guitar simply
by sitting still. Silent. They resonate art by doing next to
nothing. They just are.

And all he could ever say about them was that they were
'beautiful'. It was never enough. It will never be enough.

For there too is beauty in misery. And true misery draws
effortlessly with the pastels of truth. There is no greater subject
than the truth. We only need to experience that truth for a
moment. That moment becomes us, as much as we remain that
moment. Indelible. The beginning of genuine art. The effortless
of a poet's misery.

12

He was unsure what it was. He thought it could be a guided meditation from a previous week, but he'd been involved in many of those over the months – over the years. Something was shifting. He likened it to a game of Tetris. Where you're so focused on two shapes connecting you fail to see the build-up on the other side as those other unseen shapes marry. Points scored unwittingly. Either way, he appeared to be writing more in his Journal. Some of the material seemed very distant. Situations and individuals, he'd not thought about for a long time, and while it was comforting to reminisce, he was conscious too that the underlying theme may well be that of 'loss'.

He knew that the notion of this was an Achilles heel. He thought about that over the years, as he was trying to untie the knots of his life. He'd got to that point where he considered that the reason that he failed to maintain any type of relationship was because he didn't allow it to get beyond a certain point. For fear of rejection. For fear of getting emotionally burnt. For the simple reason that he just became bored with the illusion of living the way the game was setup. He was an emotional retard.

Going over the previous seven days he realised that he'd said little about his father. The RAF was still scratching away. The indoctrination of religion. The usual cosmic dalliance with existential pap. Really? Is that what his 'spirituality' was becoming? A 'cosmic dalliance with existential pap'. Maybe they're right – those who question 'spirituality' with a simple argument. Is it not just nice to be nice? Is that not what it all boils down to? If only it was. On the face of it – that's the easy way out. His father wasn't 'spiritual'. He offered nothing into the argument other than, 'what do you remember before you were born – nothing. Well that's what you'll remember when you're dead. Nothing'. Yeah, thanks for that Professor Brian Cox. You lazy arsed agnostic, you.

His father was an enigma.

His writing was flowing. Not with the momentum of a catharsis but literally flowing. In the flow. He'd only ever been consciously aware on a handful of occasions about the flow. That innate sense of connection with the divine essence of being. He reminded himself to write down and list those moments. It wasn't a long list, more a lexiconic conduit through which his writing would flow. At this rate, he could have enough to begin thinking about writing a book. It was happening. He'd thought about it earlier. There are two sides to every story – and somewhere in the middle is the truth. Without further ado he must head for that elusive middle ground – the centre of truth.

He was feeling buoyed by his thoughts. He knew the stories. The lies. The one-sided, negative opinions of others. Yeah, he'd done bad things. Made stupid decisions. Anyone can do the wrong thing for the right reasons – and conversely, the right thing for the wrong reasons. That's what dims the concepts of 'right' and 'wrong' – there is no such thing. It too subjective. He'll stay right here in the grey fields. Focus on the positive and the negative instead.

He had no appointments this week. No questions to face. Nothing. Sometimes he looked forward to a different perspective but often he felt like they didn't understand themselves. Over the years he'd met quite a few, with a broad range of qualifications and specialisations. Some used biros, others used expensive gifted pens to scribble down their notes. The one thing many of them had suggested was written as concisely as three letters. BDP – and every now and then he could make out some of the scrawl from the pile of previous notes. 'Borderline. Personality. Disorder'(???). The question marks were always reassuring. Keep 'em guessing. It made him smile when he read it. It was comforting to know that they thought he had a personality. Which was more than he could say for at least one ex-partner.

He'd been reading through his Journal. Surprised at what he was saying and how he was saying it. He'd made an entry and began to write in the first person. This was unusual. First person. Third person. What does it even matter? He was beginning to get frustrated with himself and the way that he was. It's not that easy to change. And it's a slow process. Reaping what you sew means waiting. It was a factor, in that he felt like he'd lost all his family. Not just his parents. Everyone. The domino effect. His mother was the Hub through which everything and everyone passed through. Her friends had become his friends – in the loosest possible way. Yeah, her sudden illness, and her death – a jolt like that is like having an accident in a very old car. The bump disturbs the rust – which is the only thing holding everything else together.

His life had been insular ever since. When she died he lost a best friend, not just a mother. A remarkable woman. God, he missed her.

Sunday

Nothing that stands before you
will become a monument
a statue or a cathedral of hate,
for all this is, all these words are
are all they have ever been,

the leaves upon branches of trees
stars within a mind of consciousness
those drips of time,
mere scars from the battles of understanding,
nothing more
than the ghosts of tomorrow.

13

Thinking abut his late mother's death occupied a lot of his thoughts. Grief is a process that has no end. It's cyclic – like everything else within nature. He had good days – he had bad days. Church bells reminded him of her. The irony being, unless there was a wedding, a funeral or a christening, she never voluntarily attended at a church whilst she was alive – certainly not in her later years. More content with a pilgrimage to Home Bargains for those 'bloody belting, you buy one - you get one free', offers. He missed her so much.

Whether he liked it or not, this weary looking town was his hometown. He'd seen it when it was vibrant and colourful, so he was qualified to opine about its current monochromatic state. Something went wrong somewhere. There was enough of it left to convince a person that it was redeemable. One thing that never leaves the town is its self-deprecating attitude toward itself. The people are its salvation.

He caught his reflection in a shop window. There was enough of himself in the mirror to confirm what he already felt. He was getting old.

He'd never really felt old until he turned fifty. That's the age. 'If you've not grown up by the time you're fifty – you don't have to'. Up until recently he'd been physically active. An odd twinge here. A creak of a bone there. An inexplicable itch around a left eye, that lasted no more than a week and then disappeared as quickly as it came. Fifty was beginning to feel like the youth of old age – forty-nine was the old age of youth. Fine lines. The unflattering reflection had confirmed this.

The train station was a hub of activity. A town's university, a glue pot for would-be academics keen to learn what the Institution wants them to know. The bridge that ran alongside the station's platforms was an excellent vantage point for spotting trains - and just far enough away to prevent you from catching one from the moment of realisation that - it's probably yours that's snaking away.

Waiting for trains had become the norm. He travelled everywhere on them – and buses; a conscious decision made during a moment of 'ethical soul searching' - and being skint. Using public transport does give a real feeling of the sense of community. You don't feel as cocooned as you are in a motor vehicle, though neither do you have to suffer the inevitable half-witted conversations from passengers talking about football. There are swings. There are roundabouts.

He was in his hometown to visit a bookshop, seeking what is arguably, George Orwell's least popular book *Why I write*. It contains 'the four great motives for writing' - according to Orwell. Fortunately, the man's own political bias was reinforced in the town and the book was available from his favourite bookstore.

On the slow train returning home, he opened the book to see where he was going wrong. He needed some inspiration. The Four Great Motives for Writing? According to George (Eric) Orwell (Blair).

1) Sheer Egoism.
   Orwell argues that a writer writes from a 'desire to seem clever, to be talked about, to be remembered after death, to get your own back on grown-ups who snubbed you in childhood, etc'. He says that this is a motive the writer shares

with scientists, artists, lawyers - "the whole top crust of humanity" - and that the great mass of humanity, not acutely selfish, after the age of about thirty abandons individual ambition. A minority remains however, determined 'to live their own lives to the end, and writers belong in this class.' Serious writers are vainer than journalists, though, "less interested in money."

2) Aesthetic Enthusiasm
Orwell explains that the present in writing is the desire to make one's writing look and sound good, having "pleasure in the impact of one sound on another, in the firmness of good prose or the rhythm of a good story." He says that this motive is "very feeble in a lot of writers" but still present in all works of writing.

3) Historical impulse-
He sums this up stating this motive is the 'desire to see things as they are, to find out true facts and store them up for the use of posterity'.

4) Political purpose- Orwell writes that, 'no book is genuinely free from political

bias', and further explains that this motive is used very commonly in all forms of writing in the broadest sense, citing a 'desire to push the world in a certain direction', in every person. He concludes by saying that 'the opinion that art should have nothing to do with politics is itself a political attitude'.

5)

He thought it best to ignore all but one of Orwell's notions as to why *he* himself chose to write. Egotism. In particular, 'to get your own back on grown-ups who snubbed you in childhood'. Why stop there? Writing's a great platform to get your own back – on anyone. Though he genuinely didn't think that this was his motivation for wanting to write. He knew it wasn't.

His journey was short, so he didn't have much time to absorb what George was talking about. He needed to read the rest of the essay. An essay neatly padded out into the size and appearance of a novella.

He disembarked the train before climbing the steps leading up to the highway, and then looked back along the train tracks from an elevated vantage point. The train he'd seen sitting on only moments earlier was snaking along its pre-determined route in the distance.

There goes the glide of yet another train.

Monday

He stopped counting the days like he stopped counting the pieces of stained glass gathered into windows. The numbers became nothing but faint mumbles when compared with the light's magnificence and the oneness from each of its colours. He thinks about her, how her voice was laughter and her laughter her voice, before the pain in a later life could no longer hide inside the powder blue of her eyes. He feels the divine when melded with the silence, just as he read that god is in the rain but not the thunder, and he is tempted to utter 'I miss you', but he pauses to marvel in what she gave him while expecting nothing in return.

Just the music is bad enough. A sublime way to twist a blade through the heart of any hope. Vivaldi's four seasons is synonymous with the Department for Work and Pensions – the D. W. fuckin' P. If ever there was a collective where the most sadistic, soulless, heartless people are gathered in employment – this must be the place. It's a generic attitude that follows the government departments around. We're the power – and you're not. The most despairing thing about it, it's the much younger individuals, those agents, that are the least aware. Most of them, you can imagine, still live with their parents. In their mid to late twenties. Having never even left home. Before they boomerang back in the fullness of time. They're the ones telling you that £12 for the last period is correct. That if that's not enough, there are emergency numbers, welfare zones within your local authority.
They're the ones that don't reply to your messages. They're the ones that sanction you when you don't reply to their messages. They're the ones. Faceless assassins. They don't even care. They're not trained enough to care. They can't even fake the sincerity. Call yourself 'public servants'. Fucking wankers.
He wasn't happy about being on benefits. Few people are.

Tuesday

During one of life's darker moments, when things were bad but not quite bad enough, he went to church.

The sound of the bells drew him in. The way each of the graveyard's headstones leaned the same way was unusual, unlike the crooked 'Cheadles' of St. Catherine's.

The preacher was dressed in Oz emerald green, speaking about Matthew five, six and seven, before a choir of eight began to sing. He didn't pay too much attention to what they were singing or what was being shot from the canon. He was there to wrap his arms around a body of faith. Feel its warmth. Wallow in the colour of its silence.

It danced its slow dance, being so careful not to step on any toes. As he left, he heard the bells once more, before they each began to fade, as if they were the one giving up on him, as if they were the one walking away.

Wednesday

Most of the town's people couldn't see that day's sun. It was too high in the sky for many to risk tilting their heads, and too intense to stare directly toward. Heat that'd absorbed into the stone of civic buildings was radiating into the streets and faint colours, once autumnal shapes inside doorways were now real people, sitting crossed legged and squinting into the confusion created when warm sunlight melds into homelessness.

It was a midweek afternoon. People doing nothing more than a notion of living. A busker was playing 3 chords on a cheap acoustic guitar. The tone of his voice was unsteady, yet the sentiment was all there. He was singing about a lost love. His eyelids were closed as he sang from the well of a bruised heart. Whoever he associated the song with, people walked past him. Few of us have the time to focus on a lost love during mid-afternoons. As he approached a dog-eared trilby, upturned on the floor, he felt inside a pocket before dropping small change, an acknowledgment to a man's burnt soul with the strength to let the world hear a festering pain. Instinctively, as the coins slapped onto smaller coins, the busker opened his eyes and thanked him with a faint smile and the slightest nod of a head. 'No worries.' They both must have thought.

As he walked further away, the resonance of those 3 chords were disturbed by a passing police car. Its two-tone sirens slicing through the melancholy and reminding himself that he was back in the town he once called home.

The few people who had any real enthusiasm left for this town were its daytime drinkers. The same men and women whose broken army are scattered throughout the four corners of this land. Each one battle weary. Each one cherishing their own nugget of faith, and each one a humble penny in the arcade of principle and opinion. The real characters. Those approaching - those at - and those beyond the tipping point. The men and women with the real stories, the fantastical tall stories, stories that in the fullness of time will morph into myth, leaving just a few to distil further into legend.

Each town has its magical places. They could be behind a single door. Deep within a local wood. They're where we'd least expect them to be, and that seems an obvious contribution to the magic.

Every now and again, possibly when the planets align, magic is tangible. It carries itself within the melodies of conversations, the peeling of church bells and those great spells of unfettered laughter. This is not the magic of sawing somebody in half or making great walls disappear, for those pastimes are illusions. The real magic comes from beyond the gauze of illusion. You just need to be looking. Some would say 'seeking'. And on this day – he was seeking.

The harsh sun was making the Parish church look like a giant Garibaldi biscuit. The armour of its sandstone walls was reflecting much of a day's light, but the outdoor heat had flowed through its open doors and filled the impressive space beyond a god's alter. Empty places of worship are much more commonplace than they've ever been. In those northern towns, when producing cotton or coal was a practice of the six-day week, there was little enthusiasm for carrying heavy sacks of religion on a seventh. Most took the less demanding option of praying at home – or the nearest public house. They still do.

Yet today was his day. In his hometown he was seeking, and he wanted answers to a small question, and as the smallest questions are deserving of the biggest answers, his question was simply once more. 'Who or What IS god'?

It was such a long time ago when he first asked himself that question. Even if he knew then, he couldn't fully understand, which, ironically, was probably why no one was prepared to explain. Not today though. There was magic in the air. That hot summer (well, a few days at least) was the catalyst for his understanding. He sat upon a Pugh furthest from the alter. Not surprised that comfort is never a factor for any of god's flock. Silent.

His attention was drawn to the church's ceiling, which had a striking resemblance to London's Westminster Abby. The detail had no doubt consumed some skilled craftsman's time. The intricate work was a show of great talent, an indirect arrow pointing to the house of religion's wealth. As grand as any of these places appear – for a man wearing flip-flops there was a great sense of his own insignificance until he scanned what was a statue of Jesus - in a tired pair of sandals. He felt less undressed. Less misunderstood.

Thursday

He slept.

Friday

The sleeping helps. It comes and it goes. Poe's, 'little slices of death'. It leaves him exhausted. A lull before a storm of creativity. Know thyself. Accept thyself. Become the Creator.

His flat was feeling like a home, though nothing much had changed since both he and his Rucksack had moved in. The one thing that had changed was his mood. A recent trip to his hometown inspired a lot of maudling thoughts. Creative but upsetting. Every time he returned there it moved him. Sometimes in a positive way – other times, more negative. Nothing really changes about the town from one day to the next, so he concluded that if the town stays the same, the only thing that does change, is him.

The Journal entries were igniting his writing. Journal entries *and* the visits. Those appointments had become routine, and some weeks he looked forward to them. He enjoyed the verbal sparring. The idea of jousting with the questions, many of which he could second guess, but some, the odd one, got through his defence and smacked him right on the nose. Sometimes he could taste the blood, but it seemed like a long time since he'd really tasted the iron from within his veins. It was the only time he spoke to anyone, answering those questions. He lied when he said he'd spoken to people in Blackpool. He kept himself to himself. Absorbed the spectacle of the Punk festival and just observed what was going on within human nature. 'People watching' reveals many things, especially from an anthropological perspective. And the criminal too. He saw at least one individual shop lifting. Tough times, tough times.

He was still convinced he was going to write a book. Not a book that would be worthy of publication – just a book. Almost like a Super Journal. One piece of work that at least displayed something of what was going on in his head. It would be fictitious. Most things that emerge from his mind have few elements of this reality contained within them. He'd considered writing a novel about Werewolves. Not least because he'd been a Werewolf in a previous life. In one of his *many* previous lives. He'd often argued that the reason he was so out of tune with this vibration is because he's still hearing the distant hum of past vibrational frequencies. The residue of those lifetimes is still soiling his pants – as it were. If that's the case, his pants must be like the starting grid of Brand's Hatch.

Though his thoughts were levelling out. He hadn't been writing poetry. Sometimes sitting down and writing poetry can be exhausting. Even writing that sounds bizarre, and few labourers would agree, or even see the similarity to 'being on the spade' and 'writing poetry'. He remembers someone once saying, 'The way you pile that wood, I'd say that you would make a good poet'. He had to think about that as a young man. It makes perfect sense now.

He decided that he was going to move his Journal along. Write longer entries. Short stories even. Erotica? Why not? The words were falling from him, and now seemed like the perfect time.

He lit a cigarette at the back door and stared toward the trees, feeling the night air against the burning within his eyes as he inhaled. As he blew out the grey debris, he thought of Dragons- and Werewolves. The usual shite. Enough to write about. And when he was ab-so-lute-ly skint. He had no choice but to write.

Things were about to become a whole lot worse – as he took the final hit of yet another last cigarette.

Saturday

The black ribbons of sidewalk in this city are filled with chewing gum stars, the small bones of dead cigarettes and a great sense of hopelessness. Darkness will eat its residents from the soles of their feet to the hearts of their faith. The only hope that resonates is through the glow of expectation and a thought of the future altered state of consciousness – all a person needs to do is to keep on moving. Don't ever stand still. Which is a notion that does little to dissuade a man from spending another day at the feast of mortality's table - but, he's here now, and it's here where he was asked - no, was begged to come. He's mindful at this point of a favourite author's saying, 'Many a good man has been put under the bridge by a woman'. That may be the case, but he makes no claim to ever being a good man. Every city is an animal.

He steps from the heat of a car, his body met with a chill that envelops him like a smog of Victorian menace - after a moment it retreats, as if embarrassed at his indifference. Who really cares for those barbs of coldness eating its way into the skeletal frame of a vagrant lay inside the doorway of a make-shift home? A face inside a hood, the palest of planets, squints a pain toward him. He squints his own in return and the vagrant turns away, back into the greater reality, that pleasant home of unconsciousness. Every city really is an animal.

As he walks along a street, he is conscious of two doormen standing beneath a bright coloured hat of neon. They look like two great bears in their heaving jackets, as he walks toward them, they stop their playful banter and look toward him, from the shine of his boots to the matt black of his stare. His stare wins. They both nod an approval that he belongs inside this dark. He walks past them both wondering just how much detail of him they would remember? The moment passes. What he is about to do is of no one's concern but his – and, of course, of hers. For now, at least.

The hotel receptionist's name was Serafina, who smiled a weary welcome that barely flopped over the line of sincerity. It had been a long day. Her eyes, in their naked state, would do little to entice a man, but the layered tones of her make-up at least embellished her stare with a provocative glance into his own tired eyes, a glance that made him conclude that Serafina would indeed be one mighty fine fuck. He considered the idea of striking up a conversation, between his awareness of consequence and an instinct to remain forgettable. He knew about her name, its origins, its etymology but was quickly distracted by a group of tourists who were getting over excited at the hotel's authentic 1920's décor, the impressive looking staircase that led from the chintz of the hotel's colourful vestibule to the diluted worth of its eighth floor furniture. 'You're in room 314', after a brief pause Serafina added 'enjoy your stay'. Accepting his room card, he glanced back in the direction of her eyes, but they were already focused on the next would-be resident, an unassuming man who smiled without noticing her name.

The door of room 314 was painted in a simple white gloss. Its gilt door fixture was well worn, and its handle was covered in tell-tale marks of frustration, scars that had been disguised with applications of gloss paint and wood filler. Signs of previous domestic situations; disputes; infidelities and trysts.

He looked along the corridor and listened. There was a noble silence coming from the hush of the thick old walls and this comforted him. Once inside he checked the time. He had an hour. Allowing for a usual trait – a few minutes more. He stepped into the bathroom and was bathed in a glow of diffused light. It made him look healthy but for a moment he cursed this light and how it exposed his thoughts but the more he caught sight of himself in the bathroom's heavy mirror, the more he was drawn to what was inside of him. He could see that faint fleck of black inside the explosive green of his iris, which was pulsing in faint dilations. Those first few tell-tale signs. He splashed cool water into the flesh of his face and stared again. He smiled and it smiled right back.

She glanced at her silver wristwatch. She was going to be late, but this was not unusual. Maybe ten minutes? It didn't matter. They'd wait. They always wait.

14

Now *that* was more like it. He read over the opening lines from Saturday's Journal entry. His attempt at a short story were taking shape. He even had names, but wondered if this was too soon? He didn't know. He didn't care. He was only writing to take his mind off another version of reality. A version that felt as real as it can get. 'In that moment', reality. 'Where you can feel it if you pinch yourself' reality. Stab yourself. Hang yourself. Under a train yourself. Poison yourself. The list is long. Reality. No. One. Gives. A. Fuck. Reality.

He thought about his next Journal entry. A list of those who don't give a hoot and why? The list would be everyone he had ever met. The reasons 'why' would be interesting. He would write that list. Soon. Very soon. Not that it mattered to anyone. He just wanted to test a theory. He was feeling annoyed. Not angry – annoyed. Historically, he'd been impatient. It was a negative and lasting trait – but over the years he'd addressed this by applying a salve of positive awareness about it. Yes, he was impatient. No, he isn't impatient. Not now. Other people still are – and he must deal with their impatience. The irony.

'Are you going mad, again?' The thought came to him out the blue. The voice. It was distinct. 'Are you going mad, again?'

He tilted his head side-to-side, feeling the grinding of tensions in and around his neck. He was tense. He couldn't remember the last time anyone had touched his neck. Massaged his neck. He couldn't remember the last time anyone had touched him anywhere. He thought deeper. Ooh yeah. What a crazy night that was. He remembered. He was going to write something about *that* night one day. He went to his Journal.

Sunday

In the hotel's vestibule, the froth of tourists had been frustrated by a delay at reception. A night shift employee, seemingly unfamiliar with the hotel's computer system explained with a simple, 'it's on a go slow', and a nod in the direction of a monitor. This seemed to buy her some time from a confused looking group. Serafina had completed her shift and was sitting at the hotel residents' bar, staring into the crystal of a balloon of Cognac, a luxury she afforded herself after any week she would describe as 'piekło na ziemi'. This week had been 'piekło na ziemi' but now there were two days off; days in which to rediscover her soul - jej nieśmiertelnej duszy.

Faking sincerity came at a cost. The heaving demands of the paying customer were becoming greater and more complex, insisting that everything was available now and not later. Just the thought of this persuaded her to order another drink. She didn't speak, she simply bounced the fine lines of her eyebrows at the bar tender. She knew he was experienced because he hadn't tried to make small talk – she smiled at how this may not be factually true. Afterall, they worked at the same hotel and more and more bar staff were becoming less and less concerned with their hotel's patrons and especially their welfare away from the hotel. It wasn't their job to enter into bursts of small talk, even with colleagues – especially with colleagues. She hated her work. Most couldn't even hold a conversation, and fewer still would be aware of the five protocols of any good discourse – let alone

93

a stimulating one, a splendid two-way communication regarding religion, sex, desires or fantasies? The Brandy was making her think and feel horny. She became increasingly aware of the pulsing between her legs. Almost embarrassingly, she looked around the bar to distract her thoughts. As she turned to pick up her glass, she became aware of a figure standing to her left. It spoke in a deep brown voice, 'a large JD with ice'. The stranger stared into the room through the polished mirrors at the back of the bar and their stares met through reflection, their gaze short enough to knowingly dart their eyes away yet long enough to become instinctively curious about each other. She recognised him and she smiled to herself at just why she remembered him but was she was aware too that her smile reached beyond her own thoughts. He felt her smile. He hadn't noticed it before, just that flash within her eyes both then and now. He'd seen that smile a thousand times before, through more than one lifetime. It was the smile that conquered kings and their armies, fell religions and faiths, the embryo of love and despair. It was all in that one smile. He took his drink from the bar and sat down. Not too close. In the same universe as that smile would be more than close enough.

She checked her wristwatch. She hadn't considered the accident. She knew she would be late - but they would wait. They always wait.

Try as he might he couldn't resist. He walked toward the bar. Again, she caught his gaze only this time sensing its true strength, standing alongside her, he ordered himself another drink. 'What would you like to drink?'

She noticed that he didn't look directly into her eyes, she probably wouldn't have either if she was asking him. She could sense this man's aura. She cleared her throat, almost timidly, 'a Brandy would be nice – a large one would be perfect.' They both recognised the double-meaning in her request and each of their smiles together with her juvenile giggle reinforced what each of them already knew. Handing her a glass seemed like the most natural thing to do. She accepted with a delicate hand and he noticed how perfectly manicured her nails were, how they were painted with a blood red varnish and how ridiculously horny they made him feel. Accepting his drink, she couldn't help but see the veins in the backs of his hands and inside his wrists. They were ridged with a life-force she quickly imagined ripping through her, stabbing at the throbbing she was now feeling between her legs. She stared into his gaze. Only this time he accepted her stare. She couldn't help but smile, again. 'So, mister three one four, tell me a little about yourself.' Her English was perfect. Her vowels were filtered through the west Slavic language tree, itself a greater turn on than her breasts. The tone in which she spoke, familiar and comforting – teasing. He leaned toward her and placing his mouth next to the shell of her ear whispered 'This may sound a little... forward, but I want to fuck you – I want to fuck you so hard and for so long that you'll beg me not to stop.' She seemed to recoil her head slightly before taking a nervous sip from her glass whilst maintaining their gaze. 'Then just why are you waiting?' 'I'm not.'

He grabbed hold of her hand which she accepted instinctively and within the space of a few short steps he had moved his grip to around her wrist, he felt a spark of resistance and increased his force a little. She relented and walked with him, by his side.

The bedside lamp was illuminated. It cast a subtle light around the room's suite. It was perfect.

'What would you like to drink?' She was tempted to say nothing but felt that in the circumstances it was only right to oblige with what little etiquette remained. 'Do you have Cognac?'

To her surprise, he did. He selected a glass from a shelf and poured a much larger measure than the one she had been drinking in the down stair's bar. He poured himself a Jack Daniels as large as her Cognac, standing facing each other - they stared intensely, drinking their drinks. Drinking each other's thoughts. There was little conversation. As if each of them was running through their own mind's eye the force of anticipation. They finished their drinks together. 'I need the bathroom.' As she turned and placed her glass on a small round coffee table, he noticed just how petit and firm her ass looked. Her long legs were encased in clear silk pantyhose and her heels were as provocative as any busy receptionist would dare to wear. He saw a bar of light shine from the bathroom as she flicked a switch. A few minutes later she returned into the room wearing all her clothes, but her smile appeared more relaxed – even more beautiful. He took a sizable gulp from the glass that he had poured. He walked toward her. Their eyes fixed, and after a moment, their gaze began to absorb into one another's being, as they dissolved into each other's soul, as they kissed for another first time.

She walked into the hotel. She was late. She was always late. Standing at an elevator door in the vestibule, she couldn't help but notice that the hotel looked beautiful. Even at over a hundred years old it still retained much of its old charm and, more importantly, most of its magic. The great chandelier; the beautiful staircase, all as they had been the last time she was here. Nothing seemed to change. That's how she liked it. Change made her feel old. As if things were evolving too

96

quickly. Slowly, slowly, slowly. Savour every moment. That had always been her philosophy – as well as a family's motto. The elevator chimed and its doors obligingly opened. She stepped inside, before the great steel mouth closed, swallowing her inside. Instinctively, she pressed '3' before she felt the gentle sway of time and after just a few seconds it fell silent again. The doors opened. In the background on a corridor wall she could see the number '3' – but it was much darker than she'd anticipated. She stepped from the elevator and turned right, walking along a corridor that had a familiar sense of loyalty and as she arrived at the room, she opened her quilted Chanel handbag and produced a gilt coloured room card. She checked the room number. 314. She was here.

She didn't knock. A single lamp threw a dim imbalance of light around the room. Three door frames formed gateways into three equal shapes of rectangular blackness. She smiled and walked through into the blackness furthest from her. As her eyes were slowly adjusting to the black, she began to remove her clothes slowly, slowly, slowly yet taking little care as to where or how they fell, now standing in the softness of her vulnerable nakedness. Searching with her hands she felt the beginning of a bed's comfort and gently climbed onto the cool sheen of its silk, her hands exploring more, she glanced the heat of a limb with her fingers, a leg, a chest, a face. She pulled at the silk sheet. 'Hello Bacchus' she whispered. 'Hello Erida, as always, you feel and smell beautiful'. Erida pulled herself across the huge bed. 'How long has she been sleeping?' 'She isn't sleeping.'

'Bacchus! You haven't already?' 'course not - we always wait Erida. I'm sure you must know that. We always wait'. 'Let me feel inside you Bacchus. Show me your heart.' They gazed into the animal of each other's eyes, neither choosing to speak or to move – they both knew why. The dilations of their pupils made their eyes appear like huge black olives, if either one of them had blinked then neither one would have noticed. They were fixed into the being of one another. He transferred the intensity of his gaze onto her mouth. Her lips apart, so perfect, ripe and full of passion. 'I've missed you', he said 'more than you will ever know''. "You always miss me Bacchus. As I always miss and yearn for you.' He smiled as he watched her lips form the sounds of those words and felt a breath of genuine sentiment absorb into his mind, before it dissolved into the rest of him, racing straight toward a heart.

Their lips touched. A moment later that passion had surged through them both. Instinctively he placed a hand around her throat and forced her backwards. He felt no resistance. She was lay on her back staring toward the ceiling, a familiar submissive pose. He kept the pressure around her throat, gripping with a frustration, an anticipation that he'd not felt for what seemed like a hundred years. Her eyes were blackening with menace. His eyes darkening with lust. He allowed her a single breath. He saw the minute narrowing of each iris. The animal was within reach. He pushed onto her throat with all his weight. The light inside the room was changing. Outside, a moon was inching its way above Venus. Her eyes were now black with fear. Two ebony orbs of reflection. Inside them he caught his first glimpse of a moon. Instinctively, he removed any pressure from around her throat. Life flowed straight back into her eyes. They flushed with dragon green anger and tease. With her first breath she whispered,

'Come to me Lykos, come to me. Devour my being, as I will devour yours.'

The light from the moon and Venus now shone through the bedroom window. Two sources of celestial, sibling light, married

98

into the magic of a full moonlight. The man Bacchus cried out in anguished pain. He placed each of his hands around the back of his own neck and knelt before Erida, who was staring with a sinister anticipation. The moonlight now washed over her. She breathed slowly and deliberately through flaring nostrils. Tide after tide of moonlight washed into the room. With each flare of a distant Venus twinkle, their forms of human shape morphed into their truest being. Bacchus would once again become the lone wolf, Lykos, Erida, now that personification of hate he must always confront with the love and a fire from his heart. As the moon continued to inch its way past their window it bathed Erida in its truest, brightest light, revealing before each of them, the real being of their individual curse. Facing toward the wolf Lykos was now nothing but blackness, a huge wall of eternal despair, cries and shrieks of desperation from tortured souls. Stones and rocks of broken hearts rained within it, the minerals of their faith and truth, momentarily sparkled in the moonlight before being enveloped in the darkest, coldest manifestation of life. Yet, in amongst the darkness, a wolf can sense the fear that comes with beauty. This in turn becomes the *real* beauty, and beauty will always be revered, if not entirely loved. Every living thing has its curse. Stare toward the darkness long enough and it weaves its curiosity into any mind. Hold darkness in your arms and you need to become the wolf to survive. Love and cherish darkness and you will never relinquish the wolf, until the curse is broken. Fire with Fire. Fire with Fire.

As the moon and Venus distanced themselves from each other's orbit, the blackness before Lykos began to take on another shape. Through the ice-blue eyes of his manifestation he once again saw Erida, her black hair now slithering around her neck and throat like a Viper, her intense stare challenging the instincts of an animal. Temptation works on many levels. She smiled at Lykos, held out her hand and beckoned him toward her. Lykos raised his head and sniffed at the space between them. She held out both her arms. 'Come'. Her voice and tone were pitch perfect. Lykos sniffed at her ankle, along the calf of her leg, in toward her inner thigh and between her legs. With both her hands she then raised his head level to her gaze and into and behind the wolf's eyes. 'My poor, poor Lykos.' Her wolf lay still beside her. Like stone exposed to running water, his curse would wear.

What startled her from unconsciousness, she wasn't sure? The room was dark with just a tissue of moonlight to aid her sight. The room was unfamiliar but the circumstances leading up to her being here were beginning to form in her mind's eye. She had worked all week. A demanding week. Gone to the bar. Had two drinks. Met a guy. Felt an immediate, animalistic attraction toward him - gone back to his room. She *so* wanted sex. She tried to remind herself just how horny she felt last night. She rolled over onto her back and tentatively felt across the bed. She touched what felt like a bare arm. Then a shoulder. Then the heat from the nape of a neck.

'Are you ok?' It was the same voice that had asked 'what would you like to drink?' the night before. Was it the night before? Was this the same night? She felt confusion for the first time. 'What time is it?'

It was the first time he'd recognised a foreign influence in her accent. 'It's nearly three fifteen - three fifteen am. Are you sure you're alright?' 'Yes, yes I'm fine. I'm sorry. Did I fall asleep?'

Before he could answer she continued 'I felt so tired, even before we met. Even before I drank - ' Her voice trailed away as he tried to hold her in his arms. She immediately felt his nakedness through her clothes. 'Excuse me one moment'. She climbed from the bed and left the room. As she passed through the doorway, he turned on a dim bedside light. The room felt still. Any shadows cast across the walls were playful shapes of imagination. None of them moved. He felt between his legs and was reassured by his hardness. Inside he smiled.

After a few moments she returned. Dressed in just plain white underwear. Her hair wilder than before. Her eyes more wanting. Her voice, subtly different. She slid back into bed before facing him. 'I don't really understand what happened last night', she whispered, ' but I still want you....' she paused 'I still want you inside me'. He gave her that smile. She returned it with a mischievous one of her own and he immediately felt his hardness twitch. As they drew themselves into each other, she felt his completeness. Not just from his groin but from his arms, his chest, his legs. She felt herself begin to throb. He began to bite into and around the nape of her neck. At her perfect nose. Her chin. His tongue stroked and brushed around her covered breasts and he was conscious that he was licking and nibbling under her arms. He sniffed and playfully bit at her face and lips. He began to smell her now. He exaggerated his sniff whilst staring into her eyes. He saw no resistance. Unfastening her bra, he leaned into her and felt a firmness that made him twitch again. He feasted on her breasts while feeding her a playful tongue that whipped and flicked at her hardening nipples. She began to moan. Those faint, embryonic moans of pleasure... 'Nisi sidera novem musae et mihi'. Serafina knew little Latin, a language she thought long dead, but the words that this man whispered into the excited swell of her were, somehow, familiar.

The heady mix of his scent, his words and his heat were only overtaken by the sensation of his fingers exploring her, as this man, this stranger, traced the contour of her naval, the bone of her hip, the line of her underwear and along her inner thigh to where her need was most raw. He pulled aside the fine white cotton of her briefs and with his whole hand he cupped her core firmly in his palm before he tentatively used a finger to explore her wet pleat. Every nerve in her body pleaded for his fingers to go deeper, she needed this. With the greatest ease, as if she were a mere leaf in the wind, he turned her body on to its front. She felt a sharp pull against the flesh of her thighs as he hurriedly removed her briefs and then lifted her hips against him, moving her down the bed in one deft move. She could feel his hot thick length press against her left buttock for a moment, before she felt herself being penetrated with an ease and to a depth she never believed possible. She had never felt so aroused. The notion of her anticipation was nothing when confronted with the reality. She felt his manhood slice deep into her. When he moved against her, she felt like a doll held in his hands, powerless, overcome, and yet she wanted more, she wanted deeper, she wanted him to tear her open. From somewhere in the void that existed outside of this bliss, she heard those familiar words 'Nisi sidera novem musae et mihi'. With the force of his next thrust she felt her head being pulled back by its hair, stretching her elegant throat and making it hard to swallow a breath. His rhythm was relentless. She could feel every ribbed vein of his cock enter and leave her, each time with a greater potency than before, a greater feeling of completeness, a greater sense of perfection; she felt a profound connection, as if each of their own physicality was designed to accept the other. Suddenly her body was flung across the bed and she was again on her back, breathless, her breasts rising and falling as her body fought for air. He stared hard at her, grabbing at her raised knee to

push back the leg that had instinctively crossed her body in front of him 'what's wrong?' 'I want to see into your soul as I'm fucking you' his words rumbled deep in his chest, 'I want to see what dwells within you'. She didn't look surprised. 'and if you do?' He whispered again, 'nisi sidera novem musae et mihi'. Before she could compose her thoughts, she felt the might of him return inside her – it forced a guttural sound from her, one that she had not known before. Then his hands were clasped at her throat, their size pushed her jaw back at an awkward angle. His thumbs pressed against the pulse in her neck, the noise inside her head was deafening as her veins screamed under the pressure of the drought. Within seconds the glow from the room was disappearing into darkness. The grip eased and the noise ended. A flood of euphoria poured through her consciousness. A brilliance of white light pulsed between her gasps for breath. His rhythm remained constant and deep, pounding inside her. She wanted to cry out to tell of the pain; instead her body released involuntary moans of pleasure. His cock was now out of her, its long, wide shaft brushing against and teasing the folds around her clit. She felt its tip, playfully nudging on the perfect spot before finding its way back into her depths. She gasped again before feeling her throat constricted once more. Anticipating the darkness, she could sense that first stirring of an ultimate satisfaction, again there was relief in the force around her neck. Without realising, she was repeatedly sounding the word 'skurwielu skurwielu skurwiel.'
He fucked her harder.

15

The brisk walk into his hometown earlier in the week had done him good. At least for a few days. Nice to intake air at its freshest. He'd gone with the intention of finding a certain book in Waterstones, and the 6-mile road-trip meant that he could test his legs - legs where he often complained about their knees having slow punctures. It was a challenge, but he was feeling healthy enough and he had nothing else better to do. He had enough money for a book. A single train journey to return. A pint. Life was good. The pubs weren't open yet. Not until he got into town, and this thought had motivated him to put added pressure on his failing knees.

He enjoyed walking into town. He enjoyed walking anywhere. It was one of the few times he didn't think too much. The route was not only familiar but nostalgic. He walked past the upstairs flat where he was first taken as a baby from a maternity home. It was once a pram shop downstairs, but like most small businesses, it had been converted into a fast food takeaway. He only spent the first few months of his life there and had no recollection about it. All his information was passed down from a late mother, who, every single time they passed the shop, would remind him, 'You used to live there'. He smiled when he thought about his mother.

He walked past a small block of flats where his aunty used to live. A place where she spent time with her late husband. He remembers going there, inside their flat. Playing indoor golf with his uncle, chipping a plastic golf ball into a motorcycle crash helmet. Watching a black and white television. And every time he thinks of a black and white television he recollects the Moon Landings. He remembers those too. Especially the first. He wasn't at school, but he was adamant that he remembers all the now iconic grainy images. The tone of the voice of the first man on the moon and some of what an astronaut said as they set foot upon earth's nearest neighbour. Apparently.

To his right, just after the bridge, a wholesale Aquarium. The same one that when he left school, he failed to turn up for a job interview because he'd overslept. Life could have been so different. Those sliding door moments. He imagined himself standing inside. Passing on learned information about Angel fish and Terrapins. Yeah, life could have been so much different. He thought about his pet tortoise. His first and only reptilian pet. He remembered the fondness with which he used to feed it lettuce. An eager mouth snaffling green leaves. It was unfortunate that for a creature that'd been around for over 200 million years, it didn't last a single winter in his young hands and under the guidance of two of the most ill-informed parents ever. It was thrown in a bin, as a mum thought it was dead at the height of its hibernating period. Those things can live a hundred years. It could still be chomping on iceberg lettuces now. Watching High Definition television and marvelling at the changes in its extended mortality. But no. Ignorance often equates to death.

The town hall clock came into his sights. The phallic timepiece of a northern town. And it told the right time. At least twice a day. His mind started to wander. He was thinking about the recent Journal entry from Saturday. It fell out of him. It was

105

inspired by a trip to Manchester and to the Britannia Hotel. He simply mapped one version of events onto another, and as he replayed that over in his mind's eye, he was seeing a film with both 'real' characters and cartoon characters. Like Mary Poppins. He wasn't sure what was occurring, but since his most recent session of conversations, he was beginning to see things vividly. It was just a case of deciding what was real and what was not?

The most recent sessions were helping. He may not show it, but he had a healthy respect for the patience and the understanding of all those involved. Yeah it was their job, but you can get a good plumber or a bad plumber from the sea of plumbers– and this guy knew all about his ball valves.

The room smelt of Sandalwood. It came as a bit of a shock. He was expecting something less natural, the familiar smell of institution.

'Good afternoon'.

The interviewer sounded determined. Focused.

'How have you been these last few weeks?'

A standard 'around the houses' introduction.

'Yeah, I've been Ok'.

'Right. Well, we'll crack on because there's a lot to get through today.'

That sounded ominous.

'I've been going over the notes that were made by your previous... ad-vi-sor'. He was reluctant to say 'advisor'. Weirdo.

'...and some of those made by me during these last few months -'

This really does sound ominous.

'They mentioned your Journal, and just how much you rely on it to transfer some of your thoughts into tangible words. Many of those thoughts are not necessarily real – or rather, some of what you write is not real. It never has been. The writing is real. What you write about is not'.

'I'm sorry, you're confusing me now.'

'When you write your Journal… ok, *why* do you write your Journal. Is what you enter real? Did it happen? For example, you write about the Royal Air Force – did that happen?'

'Some of it. I write. You're allowed to imagine beyond what really occurred. Refrain from telling some truths. Often, the truth is the one reality we cannot cope with. Sometimes it's too much, but most of the time it isn't nearly enough'.

'Where are you now? Right at this moment. Who are you now? Right now?'

I wasn't expecting this today.

'I know who I am. I don't see myself confined by a name or a moniker. I may have been named or baptised as, Daniel Halland but I asked myself a long time ago – is that really who I am? Afterall, we can each change our name. Change our environment. Be somebody else with very little effort. Then when does Daniel Halland stop being Daniel Halland? When do they start to become whatever it is the think they want to be? What does even *being* that new 'person' mean? How does the new differ from the old? We can always be all things. In fact, we are. Invent yourself, then reinvent yourself. And again. And again. No matter how many times you do that, it's never enough unless you understand what it means to be you. Know yourself. Accept yourself. It's a mantra I use. Often'.

'Do you know who you are?'

'Better than that…I understand why I am'.

'Ok, who are you - and why?'

So far he hadn't scribbled anything down. This was unusual.

'I am you. I am them. I am what I would loosely term… 'infinite consciousness. A small part of the divine creation and as such, I too am infinite. Saying that is one thing. Feeling it – another. I mean, literally feeling it. The ironic thing about it is – and I used to not get this part – I was so close to 'getting it' I thought I got it. I could taste it, smell it, hear it, even touch it - but *never* saw it. When I finally did see it – I realised that I didn't need eyes to see it. That's how crazy it is!

He still wasn't scribbling anything down.

'What is it you see?'

'Believe it or not… I see love. Not those wisps of emotional love that are smoked from the controlled pipes of needs and wants; pure undiluted, universal love. The one thing that the power knows about but cannot control. So instead, they distort it. They interfere with its true vibrational frequency and create divisions, distortions and negative imbalance above and beyond the polarities of nature - '

Finally. A scribble.

'- and consciousness. I feel 'consciousness'. Literally, feel it. Divine consciousness. I feel it in the trees. Within water. The sky. The clouds. Everything. Somedays it can be overwhelming - '

'In what way?'

'Just that feeling of being smothered with love. Everything *is* love. Once you're through that veil of forgetting what it is, that what we innately know and understand – boom! It's there'.

I said too much. Carried away again. They *did* ask. If they ask – you show.

'Do you ever not feel real. Unreal, as it were?'

'I do. I know it can sound crazy and that's the paradox. There are many levels of consciousness that exist. Many levels of reality. Sometimes those levels meld with another consciousness that isn't directly next to it. It isn't linear. A rainbow as the colours meld. When does one colour become the next? It's obvious that the colour changes, but the actual point of the change, that transcendence, is where? That point. There. What exists practically. Exists metaphysically. The universe doesn't begin or end at the end of our nose. That's ridiculous. I once used to think that it did, though. We are the universe. A part of it – not apart from it'.

I'm sure I saw him stifle a yawn.

'I don't talk about this often, but it's nice to talk about it occasionally. It took me a lifetime to work it all out'.

'What did you work out?'

'That I am the Creator. You are. We *all* are'.

'We're all god?'

'Pretty much. Except for one ex-partner. She's Satan'.

I had to lighten the mood of the room somehow. The smell of Sandalwood had vanished.

He scribbled. Not with the world's most dangerous or expensive pen. It was a Bic biro. I wasn't sure if it influenced what words he was writing down. I imagined that it didn't.

'Ok, let's go back'. He appeared to move forward in his seat.

'You have no belief in god?'

'I have no belief in anything. I have faith'.

'Faith in…?'

'In what I've witnessed. In what I've felt'.

'What have you witnessed. What have you felt?'

'I've seen lots of things. On their own they made little or no sense, though as you begin to piece them all together, they make all the sense in the worlds'.

'The worlds?'

'Yeah, the worlds. There's more than one world in the universe that facilitates existence'. Even as I said it, I could see that he thought I was crazy. Maybe it was me?

'Have you been to any of these other worlds?'

'I'm pretty sure that throughout the course of my existence, I have. Though I have no distinct memories. Not like the memories I have of previous incarnations upon this world'.

The interviewer shuffled forward again.

'Such as?'

'Well, through my journey, I remember being the ocean. The trees. The sky. A bird. An eagle. A snake. An Egyptian slave. A wolf… I quite enjoyed my time as a wolf. And more recently, I was a German SS soldier. Though I never had chance to tell my grandfather. He would've gone mad'.

I could see that he didn't know where the joke started or finished. He was still considering the bit about the ocean and the sky.

'How distinct are these memories?'

'Very distinct. Very real. As real as me and you sitting here.'

He scribbled before sitting back in his chair.

'I want you to write a story…'

'I've just written something in my Journal. About Werewolves. About the personification of darkness. It was quite erotic, and for somebody that considers themselves an asexual, it was quite revealing….'

'I want you to write a story about love'.

'A love story?' This was getting weird.

'Yes, a love story'.

Before he could explain any further, I was formulating an idea in my mind.

'It doesn't have to be too long, but write it in the first person'.

Better still.

'Ok. How long does it have to be?'

'I'll leave that up to you'.

I enjoyed his games. I knew exactly how long it would be.

I couldn't wait to get home.

'Just one more question. You've explained 'what' you think you are, but you haven't really touched upon 'why' you are?

'I'm in the process of showing you. Showing everyone'.

16

Monday

It was the first time in a long time that he'd missed a day writing in his Journal. The last session had taken a lot from him, but also given him some inspiration to write. Some real purpose. He'd started writing a little poetry.

will these words ever reach from their page
would the fingers of their letters grab
at the air
or stroke the beauty of a stillness?
spectres of meaning can hide
within the shadows,
never tasting sunlight or weighing the colours
of hurt and loss.
He'd got to that age.
That age where
the abuse starts to morph into
black cats,
black cats
walking past his feet.
Not the old age of youth
but the youth of old age
no line to separate the two.
No fissure.
No mark.
Just time and the wonder of space.

It wasn't brilliant, but it was a start. Poetry is situated at the back of one of those rooms furthest away in his mind. It takes an effort to get there. A labyrinth of ladders and snakes, but the only real fight worth fighting. To wrestle those words from the beast is an effort; beauty isn't given up easily by those that carry the swords of vanity.

He went to a drawer and picked out his Journal from 1983. He flicked through the year's pages, as he'd done many times. The 8th February 1983 was a Tuesday. Kajagoogoo were 'Too Shy', he had sex twice and drank 2 pints of mild. Other than it being Ronald Reagan's birthday, that summed up the day. Boring. Even the sex. *Especially* the sex.

That wasn't the date he was after. He knew what happened on that date. He was after another date. *The* date. What he did know, in between the recent upheaval of moving to a new flat, was that next year was a significant milestone in his life. In the year 2020 he will be 20,000 days old. He needed to get a move on. He had to sort his life out. His writing. Not the new. The old. The interviewer had asked him to write a love story. Why? He had pile after pile of papers and old computer folders of his writing. Most of which was written at a time when he thought things were on an even keel. He rarely did what the interviewers asked of him – he knew this was another indication of his life's issues. Few people enjoy being told what to do – and those who do, usually harbour some sort of kink.

He rummaged through one of the two drawers in his bedroom before quickly retrieving a black hard drive. Back in the day 250 gigs was a lot of memory – and this storage device was the size of a typical paperback book. Contained within it – if the thing still worked – was just about everything that he had typed into a computer device over the last twenty years, but in particular - the last fourteen years. He knew there was poetry on there, especially in relation to his time spent in the police. Time spent falling out of love. In love. Becoming a father. Becoming an estranged father. In short – there was a lot of emotion channelled into that storage device. He was curious as to just what exactly he may find? It may even reveal something to himself. Afterall, he isn't the same person. He doesn't feel like the same person. And show me a man that's the same at 50 – as he was at 36 - and there's a man that's wasted 14 years of his life.

He fumbled with the hard drive. After sorting through several leads, it was obvious that he didn't have the lead that powered it. He made a mental note of the type of 12v flex required.

That kind of work was exhausting, rummaging through drawers. He went to the back door and lit a cigarette. As he inhaled a great hit of nicotine, he stared back at the inanimate hard drive. Many of his thoughts were inside that piece of technology – and pictures too. Thousands of pictures of a family. Friends. Lovers.

He didn't know whether the idea of resurrecting a past was a good idea. Plenty of people do it. Nostalgia. He was just troubled in case it reminded him of how far he may have fallen. He checked himself. It will remind him of just how far he has travelled. He flicked the cigarette into the garden soil.
He had to find *that* lead.

Part II

17

It was just after midday on a late summer afternoon.
It was in a northern town. It was raining. I fell in love.

Her eyes were deep, deep blue. They concealed some of her
madness, but nowhere near enough.
I saw beyond it. I saw her past. I felt her magic.
I knew there was no lie in her fire.

'Don't look at me', I said.
She stared over my shoulder, leaned toward me and whispered
 'It's too late.'
We both knew she was right.
We each recognised one another from previous incarnations.

Its beer garden is magical. It plays the kitchen's role at house
parties, where the coolest of the cool are hanging out; smoking
exotic cigarettes and a little green, discussing anything from alien
invasions to the etymology of words. Never football.
        The reality is, the garden is a small space forged between
four joining sides. It works. It *is* magical. On the perfect day,
when everything is in its place, you will feel it. You will hear it.
You will see it. Fuck, you will even *be* it.

That's where it began. Where it really started.

Wednesday

I am nearly fifty years old. In this illusion life began at forty. A mid-life insurgence of irrational thinking and behaviours were the catalyst. At forty I stopped being who people thought I was. Now, over a decade later, I am ready to begin again.

Yes, it was magical. And spells are magic too. It was a combination of our energies that created that spell. Woven together through many lifetimes. I am over nine hundred years old. Sounds unbelievable? Read the Bible. Jared and Noah. That kind of age.

She is over ten thousand years old. Sounds ridiculous. Sounds crazy. That's just how it is. Magic can last forever.

No more mister nice guy. I'm coming for you. You know who you are. I cannot wait to see you, old friend.

The rain was shooting against a window. It was cool outside but enough of a sash was open to allow cigarette smoke to float through and beyond. I didn't like smoking in bed. I hadn't done it for years. Even smoking inside a house seemed unnatural. Unhealthy. Toxic.

She lay at the side of me. Rolling a joint. Her measure and routine, I knew I had a couple of minutes before she offered me a chance to get high. I'd take it. Sometimes you've got to run just to stand still. Right now, I didn't want to be motionless in spirit. Not only that, there's some good green going around these days – so I'm told. If I smoke it - I'm usually sick – or start to trip. I can cope with the nausea. I used to panic with the trip. Now, I'm just thankful of anything that gets me out the house.

'I've been having some crazy, vivid dreams.'

She looked at me. She didn't say anything but threw me a look that said, 'you *are* a crazy, vivid dream.'

'Here.' She handed me the well-rolled spliff. Not perfect. Practical.

I lit it and inhaled on the bud that I'd heard her grind. There wasn't much tobacco in there. All you could taste was the animal. The bit she insisted she liked the most. She told lies too. I lay my head back on the pillow and stared at the ceiling. I'd done that before. If staring at ceilings was an Olympic sport, I'd be a medallist.

'What were you dreaming about last night? You were restless -'

'I don't know.' I lied. I positioned my head into the comfort position, before starting to see purples and blues as I closed my eyes. Nothing too bright – but lighter than the dark.

'I was along the astral. I couldn't get back at one point. I was challenging myself to wake up, but I couldn't – I kept going and going. Almost without having the ability to do so. Like skiing within a dream – not through skill, just by luck and

119

circumstance. Then I felt like I was flying through space and time. Yeah, it's all coming back to me. And I was back in that pub. Astral to the pub. Seems like a natural progression. I met someone who was over ten thousand years old. I knew them. An old flame. I was as old as Noah.'

She didn't say anything, simply held her hand out to take the rest of the spliff from me. It was hers after all. I hate the stuff. Sends me crazy.

The curtains were open. The rain had stopped. It looked bright outside. I showered. Changed back into the clothes I was wearing the night before and set off for home. I had to check myself that home wasn't too far way. That I had the means to get back. No amount of ruby red will get me home quicker.

'Thanks for last night', I wrote on a wipe board on the fridge. Nothing happened. We both fell asleep. That's what friends do – and what friends don't do. She'd gone off to work. I was to see myself out. Make sure the cat flap wasn't blocked. Check the oven was switched off – if I ever did use it. She'd left me a cigarette on the kitchen table. As I fumbled about for a light – I recalled her name.

The cigarette tasted bitter. I was about to leave. Checked myself before going back to the wipe board, adding an 'x' under the word 'night'. It made me feel better. I couldn't see her again. She was getting too much. I wanted a woman who was Ok with being with me just 5% of my time. I never know what that really means? I guess I'm just always looking for an excuse. Isn't everyone? There's no place like home. There's no place like home...

It was still early. Some of the birds were singing. Like Picasso once said, 'You don't stop to ask what the birds are saying – you just enjoy that they sing.' That's him trying to explain his art, right there. Any art. Too many people are quick

120

to condemn creativity. 'Those who don't create art will never understand art'. Thanks again, Hank.

The sky was battleship grey. The last of the rain was disappearing and dry patches were appearing in the tarmac. Puddles would all soon be gone. Gone where? Transferred their worth Their energy. Into something else. Something new.

A hint of green was flowing through that room in my mind. Sometimes it felt like a nine-headed hydra, Medusa's crown of snakes. I can see Lilith too, spitting her venom; disguised as tears. A demon of temptation. It dwells within us all. She's good. Determined. She's been with me such a long time. A negative entity. Her and Zozo. What a couple. One on each shoulder. It starts to rain again. A few spots. Enough to make me tilt my head to the heavens. God is in the rain. He really is. I need him now.

Fuck. I'm still high. The bus is a giant green reptile. Its eyes burning white. Let it pass. Let it pass. Let it pass.

I just need to keep walking. So, I walk. Nowhere is a long way but we all get there soon enough.

18

My mother is dying. My father too. Though they're fading at different rates. It's not over until it's over – and it's just about over. You can see where the life once dwelled. You can see where each of them kept their hope. Those places are eroding away. There will soon be no room for any version of hope. The last of Pandora's box.

I think that they're both looking the wrong way down a telescope's lens. There is little hope at the feast of mortality's table. Their hope should be focused elsewhere – and even then, it's faith that cultivates hope. My father doesn't appear too concerned. I think he knows more than he ever lets on.

He saw god a few weeks ago. As he Stared unblinkered toward the corner of a room and its ceiling.
'What are you looking at', I asked.
'god.' He wouldn't stop staring.

He was eighty years old and it was the first time I'd heard him say the word 'god'.

Better late than never – or so dad hoped?

Friday

They're both dead now. I can't write anything. I'm too numb. If I did write anything it'll be in the months that follow. I have no ability to think. To feel. To pray. I'll light a candle. She can become its light – the light can become her. I'll hear her voice in this house. She lived here long enough. I can hear her in the kitchen. No. That's next door. I'll hear her soon enough. All I must do is lay here. Keep the light burning. Wait until the feeling comes back. Wait for god to appear from the corner of another room.

I really need to sort my shit out. It's the year 2015. My parents are dead. My family is shattered. Lost in its own confusion. In its own levels of self-preservation. Its own selfishness. This Journal has been neglected. Too many holes and missing days. Looking back over the days of the last few years, it seems I've only lived a fraction of my days. Words don't define a man. Actions do. Maybe I'm 'doing' much more than I'm 'saying'. Maybe.
That'll be a first.

I take some responsibility for that. I must. I'm the father figure now. I know I can't though – there are gaping holes in the story. I need to write it all down. How I see it. People think I'm weird anyway. They think I drink too much. They judge me. They don't know anything other than what they think they see. The truth hurts – but there is nowhere after that. It's taking any power away from individuals. They have nowhere to go. It exposes them for who and what they really are. Most cannot cope with that. They're so far away from the truth that it's too much for them. The journey back toward truth. Away from the distortions that are created around them, they absorb them all.

123

Hook – line and sinker. It saddens me. Their notion of love. It's corrupted them. They cannot admit it. They gravitate toward like-minded people. They enable each other to carry on behaving in the ways that they're comfortable with. It's what creates the illusion of divisions between us. It is a game, though. It's just a game. A ride. It's just a ride. 'Oh, hiya Bill'.

Sunday

Anyone who has lost a parent will understand. Though few people lose both parents in quick succession. It happens, you do hear about it. One dying just after the other, 'of a broken heart'. I'm sure that can happen, but in my father's case, I'm not so sure. I'd like to believe that he did. I wasn't there when he died. Though to be honest, a significant part of my father died many years before he passed away in hospital. He saw it all too late.

19

It was a sunny day in April 1994. The few clouds were unseasonably white and the colour behind them was postcard blue. It was a beautiful day to become a father.

A side room in the hospital was an archetypal space in which to bring new life into a world. It was a time when father's to-be were encouraged to witness the birth of children, and all that came along with that. The contorted face of an about-to-be mother. The determination. The whole natural and exhausting process of squirting life between realms. What they didn't tell me – a cop of three and a half years – was that the least traumatic end from which to spectate was from a mother's shoulders looking back toward the long grass. That way, you're there – but there's something left for an imagination. A man who had witnessed post-mortems, sudden deaths, horrific injuries at Road Traffic Accidents, wasn't going to be perturbed by the natural events of a childbirth.

Much of that birthing process is still burnt onto my ageing retinas. Like witnessing a car accident in slow motion. The beauty of life unfolds over a lifetime – the beauty of birth in the final minutes of a labour. Both mother and new-born child came through the experience relatively unscathed. I cut the umbilical cord and winced at its thick resistance to surgical scissors. Men are pathetic.

I was a father. A husband. A professional person. I had a mortgage, but apart from that - 'debt until death' - life seemed good.

Thursday

I became a father today. Even writing that sounds bizarre. She's beautiful. Just like her mum. They're both staying at the hospital overnight. I'm going out. Wetting the proverbial.

It was around two weeks later. April's weather is unpredictable, but I remember it was raining. The telephone rang. It was on the windowsill in the bay window of a living room. I was looking outside as I picked up the telephone.

'Hello?'

There were two magpies bouncing on the lawn of a front garden. 'At least they're having fun', I thought, waiting for an inevitable reply. The line was open. I could tell. After a couple of seconds, I heard the click of a receiver being put down.

One of the magpie's stared toward me before it flew away. The other remained, shamelessly pecking for worms.

20

The blue lights were always exaggerated in the mirrors of wet and rain. Patterned reflections from a road's puddles that you never got to see in the dry. Even the raindrops that gathered on the roof of a car became blue-light strips. Very NYPD.

I arrived outside the building. A block of maisonette flats. I was looking for number 16 and there it was. Surprisingly displaying its number. They had a habit of being removed once the postman knew where to drop the mail.

I was the first at the scene, but I knew I wouldn't be the last. 'Violent Domestics' are never short of patrols volunteering to attend, especially when it's wet (cold) and dark.
I repeated the initial radio message back in my head.
'Any foxtrot one patrol for a violent domestic, believed male armed with a knife…'

I was about to ask the police radio operator, her name was 'Mandy', if any more information had become available. Any 'Sitrep' updates. Situation reported updates etc etc blah de blah de blah.

*When I finally do write this book. I need to avoid writing about the police. It bores me! I need to tell this though, to try and give it some measure of perspective. A dipstick for the barrel of any madness that ensues.

In the end I said, 'At scene'.
At least the other cops knew that I was there.

The male believed to be armed with a knife turned out to be, 'a deranged head-the-ball violent mother fucker' - armed with a knife, who had an innate sense of hatred towards anything resembling the police. He also had impeccable timing. Leaving the ground floor flat just as I arrived. I was wearing full uniform. Stab-vest. Side-handled baton. CS gas. Kwik-Kuffs and a frown.

He was semi-naked but had an air of assurance that I imagined only comes when you're high, subsequently fearless and the custodian of a huge machete.

'Come near me ya cunt and I'll fuckin' stripe ya.'
I reacted by extending my baton and fumbling about for the CS gas. I had, on occasions, forgot to take gas out on the streets with me. I walked along the pathway toward him. It was at the sort of pace you walk toward anyone carrying an 18" blade. I was conscious of other blue lights behind me. The cavalry had arrived. Though it was possible that I was going to have to take one for the team. Or lose one. An arm. A leg. A scrotum.
I bellowed at him, 'Put. The. Knife. Down!'
He remained with the blade, angled in a grip of his right hand.
'Do us all a favour and put the knife down and step toward me.'
I said, in a more hopeful than instructive tone.

I didn't know how many officers where behind me at this point but judging by his expression, there were too many for him to chop and splice his way through. Surprisingly he threw the knife to the front of himself, before showing everyone that his hands were empty. He was instructed to kneel. The usual format you see on the Tv. Safe for the cops. Safe for the perpetrator. Once you've got them cuffed and free from any items that they could harm or cause a danger to themselves (or any other), that's when you place them into the back of a suitable police vehicle. Then at that point, but not restricted to, that's where some cops ~~beat the shit out of 'em. Or as it was known back then. They~~ formally advise the alleged offender.

Over the years I've had some mileage out of that man. The 'Violent and Deranged Man Armed with a Machete', had stabbed his partner three times and tipped a fanciful collection of tropical fish onto a carpet during the process. I'd received a Chief Constable's Citation of Merit (CCCM) – or something as equally worthless, and an endless war story to embellish. I didn't know it then, but that incident probably did lend itself toward some form of PTSD. That and being forced to watch United play every other weekend.

21

Sunday

I'm beginning to realise why I don't make as many Journal entries as I used to. I'm always writing at work. Notebooks. Statements. Maybe that's just the process that I feel that I must do._Need to do. It doesn't matter what you write, just as long as you're writing?

Some dick came at me with a machete the other night. Fuckin' prick. And some fucker is playing silly games. Phoning up and then putting the handset down. Three times it happened. Though not for over a week. Mong.

Monday

The Police Force is changing. It's changing from a 'force' to a 'service'. More 'customer' based. What a load of bollocks. This is the beginning of the end for many. Me included.

I can see how it all works. Those wheels-within-wheels. The rhetoric. The semantics. The language. It all distils into one thing. The power. You can see how the power is distributed. You can see through those that know. Those that understand. Not because they've worked it out but simply because they've been made aware. Often before they joined the police. Family members. Members of associations – not least the freemason fraternity. Power. Knowledge. Awareness of the game. All played out in front of you. The Police. The Courts. The Law. The Governments, and above all them – the *real* power. Unidentified but there in the shadows. Tentacles everywhere. Distortion of truth.

I'm inside the Whale's belly. Jonah. I'm inside the Trojan Horse. Odysseus. I'm that close to it - I can smell it. I can feel its energy. It's nauseating. Not to everyone. Some gravitate toward it. To them it smells like sugar. Sweet apples. Candy floss. It makes me sick.

I swear by almighty god that the evidence I shall give, shall be the truth, the whole truth, and nothing but the truth.
The truth? The truth *is* truth. It doesn't begin or end with trite declarations on an oath to power. The relationship between 'honesty' and 'truth' – a person can be completely honest and

not even be in the same room as truth. I've seen the game. They practice the sincerity of honesty – convince a person you're being honest, and most people will assume that you're always telling the truth. Some police constables don't even know what the truth is - but they're honest. Those who break through – who work it out - but choose to remain - choose 'security' over 'freedom'. Mandela once said, 'If you choose security over freedom - you will end up with neither'. Freedom of mind. Freedom of will. Soiled by the notion of security.

Once you join organisations such as the police, you sign away a significant part of yourself - and many don't even realise. They're too focused on what they believe they are. Protectors. *Protecting People – Fighting Crime*. On one level – that is exactly what they do. On *one* level.

There are many layers. It isn't what I imagined. I was naïve. I should have gone into social work. I should have avoided the establishment altogether. The negative.

22

The liights went out tonight. It went dark becose of miners. Mum put candles in the house. I like it when it is dark and no liights.

Daniel Halland Aged 7

23

"It was a bright cold day in April, and the clocks were striking thirteen."

It really *is* the year 1984. I'm working in a factory. There are clocks everywhere. You clock in. You clock out. There's no slacking. If the machine breaks down, we have to make boxes. A machine can't make the boxes. It can make oil filters. It can make air filters - but it can't make boxes. The machine starts up again. So do we. Now there are no boxes being made. Surely we'll run out of boxes? That was me – thinking outside the box(es).

The factory is huge. The last one burned down. It was too old and somebody made a mistake rewiring the new wires, and the whole thing burned down overnight. They called him 'Butfahim'. He was an Indian man. He's working in the new factory and when he walks past the women say, 'Ooh, but for him we'd still be at the old factory'. The women liked it better at the old factory. The women always like to complain. If they're not complaining – they're laughing. I like working with them. They're funny.

I enjoy reading the first lines in books. I don't know where that comes from? Everything has got to start somewhere. It really is April 1984. It's not cold. It's not bright. Today is Sunday 22nd April. It's Easter Sunday. I'm not Winston Smith.

I don't have many books. Jaws by Peter Benchley sits on a bookshelf. Stig of the Dump by Clive King, C.S Lewis's - The Lion the Witch and the Wardrobe - and now 1984. Not a great library for an eighteen-year-old. Books take too long to read. I always preferred comic books. Queen reads every day. You cannot move downstairs for the piles of her books. Catherine Cookson. Sidney Sheldon. I've never seen her read a bible.

'The great fish moves silently through the water.' I only read the book after I'd seen the film. The film was unconvincing. It was difficult to be frightened of anything that bent in the middle the way the 'giant shark' did. The music is the scariest bit. The book has some great lines though.

"Look, Chief, you can't go off half-cocked looking for vengeance against a fish. That shark isn't evil. It's not a murderer. It's just obeying its own instincts. Trying to get retribution against a fish is crazy." I couldn't agree more. Leave the fish be.

Now I'm older, 1984 (the book) is beginning to make some sense. It's a pity I can't make any sense out of the real world. Whatever that is?

Off to bed. Monday tomorrow. Making filters is tiring work. I can't see myself doing this until I'm sixty-five. Sixty-five? Nineteen.

24

The Miners are kicking off. They're always going on strike. I don't know too much about it. A policewoman has been shot and killed outside an embassy in London. I quite fancy the idea of going in the police. Not to get shot and killed. That's unfortunate. That's London. If I was going to join the police – I'd be a policeman in Manchester. I've not heard of many police getting shot there.

I've got another book. This one is a dictionary. It's huge. Big enough to use on the corner of my bed where the leg has broken off. I still don't know how that happened?

There are 3, 200,060 people unemployed. Not working. How do they even measure that? Who are these people? Everyone I know is working. Mum, Dad, Sister, next door neighbours. Those across the road. Everyone.

That dictionary came in useful. I heard a word on the radio. I like how it sounded. Some words sound better than others. Loquacious. My mum is loquacious. I looked through more of the dictionary. It's interesting. Better than 'World in Action'. I'll usually go and whack one off when that comes on the tele. I really hope Andrea doesn't read this. I think I'm falling in love with her. I might write a love letter.

Sunday

After work this week I went straight out. I drank dark mild. I must have had about 8 pints. Apparently, that's a gallon. 'Too much for an 18-year-old.' That's what my mum says - but she doesn't drink. I ignore what my dad says. He says, 'you've only had enough when the ambulance comes.' Surely nobody can drink *that* much? I've found a new name I can call my dad. A 'Cochaloorum'. It means he's 'a self-important little man'. To be fair, he's not that little - but it sounds good – so I'll use it.

You don't get much space in this diary to write anything during the week. Saturday and Sunday, there's enough room there – but the last few weeks I've not been doing much on Saturday or Sunday. So, what I'm writing isn't necessarily what I've done today. I don't even know *why* I'm writing? 1984 must have some significance if George Orwell can write about it in 1949. I'm writing about 1984 in 1984 - and that doesn't seem like much of a challenge. I guess if and when I read this back – in say – the year 'Deathrace 2020', things will be a whole lot different. I certainly hope I will be. I might even be dead. If I'm not – at the very least - I'll be an old man.

Tuesday

I've been seeing her a while now. It's 'on and off'. I don't even know why it's 'on and off' but it is. Then it isn't. My mum thinks I should settle down. I'm 18. Just because she got married at 19 – she thinks that's the norm. I know people in their mid-twenties who haven't even thought of getting married. I know I'm getting fed up with work. I can't imagine working there much longer but I don't know what else to do? I don't know what else I *can* do?

I should have paid more attention at school. Not dicked about. I told my dad the job I was doing was 'semi-skilled'. He laughed and said, 'you're either skilled or you're not.' That was followed by the usual story of his young life as a, 'Sheet Metal Worker'. I scoffed at him, 'I don't want to bend metal for a job or make shapes out of tin. I'm going to do something proper.' 'Like putting seals into air filters?' 'Like joining the police.' That shut him up. He wanted to go in the police – but he'd suffered from Tuberculosis as a younger man. I think he knew it was never going to happen.

Just read today that the age limit for joining the police has risen from eighteen and a half – to twenty-one. It's looking like I'll be making filters longer than I'd hoped. Dad was right.

Friday

The miners are still on strike and there's been some scuffles and riots shown on the tele. Liverpool are still winning European Cups. Humanity is flying off into space and coming back again in a Shuttle. We'll be living on the moon before I'm thirty. Not me. It's bad enough living here. There must be somewhere out there in the universe that's better than here? Like, 'Close Encounters'.

I've started writing poetry.

25

It wasn't the King's farthing when I joined. It was £30. Doesn't seem like a lot now. It wasn't a lot back then. It was enough. That's what happens – it's always *just* enough.

I joined the Royal Air Force Police in the spring of 1985, as much through chance as endeavour. The Army careers office was a welcoming place. They usually are when you're standing on the right side of the fence. The military police sounded far too fantastical. Far too regimented. The Army Corporal was talking to another young man who was dressed in civilian clothes and sitting at a desk *like* a civilian. This adolescent glanced in my direction, and I saw just a flash of anxiety in his eyes. It was enough.

The Royal Air Force Corporal had much more hair than I had anticipated. Members of the forces had short cropped hair, but this guy had a dark mop sitting on top of his head. He felt less intimidating.

'Can I help you?'

'I'm here to talk about the Royal Military Police. Get some advice. Find out a little more about it.'

'Are you joining the army?'

'I don't know. I have some questions. I wanted to join the real police, but the age limit's just risen from eighteen and a half to twenty-one. I'm eighteen and a half. So, I am thinking of the military police, as a ... as a ...stepping stone ?'

'Take a seat. Let's talk about the pretend police.' He smiled as he said that.

The Royal Air Force Corporal went on to explain all about the Royal Air Force Police. The RAFP. The 'Snowdrops' was the polite word he used. He explained how they were recruiting for several trades, and the RAFP was one of them – subject to passing an entrance examination. He continued to sell the vocation to me, but I was already drifting into a future reality, and imagining myself dressed as a Royal Air Force Police NCO and not as a Royal Military Policeman. The blue uniform was much more endearing than the Army's camouflage fatigues. In the time it'd taken listening to him talk about the Falklands 'conflict', I was pencilled in for an entrance examination and assessment in Manchester. Four weeks later, I was at a Lincolnshire airfield marching into the unknown. Six weeks after that, I was marching in time, together with a distinctive collection of other young men. Fourteen weeks after *that* , I received my RAFP Non Commissioned Officer stripes (Corporal) and was sent into the crazy world of the real Royal Air Force. **Per Ardua ad Astra.**

The whole training experience was surreal. One minute I was involved in the manufacturing of Air and Oil filters inside a northern factory – and the next I was playing a significant role with a part responsibility in the security of the UK's nuclear weapon deterrent. The disparity seemed too great. It was – but I was too young to care.

Part III

26

The darkness was overwhelming. Total darkness. Unless you've experienced it – you cannot even imagine.

That's what he was feeling. He was conscious of *being* conscious. Awake within total darkness. Silent. Consciousness. He felt nothing else. No sensation of heartbeats. No feeling of sight, of limbs, of environment. He thought he was dead.

That thought alone was the spark. He felt no panic. He felt no pain. What he did begin to feel – was the light. Brighter and brighter. Slowly at first. The typical light of a day's dawning. Brighter and brighter and brighter. Then he began to feel *it*. For the very first time. He wasn't sensing the brightness appearing from any particular direction, and yet the sensation was now everywhere; where the blackness felt like emptiness, the light was beginning to feel whole. In an instant, and along with the increasing brightness, he felt the euphoria. He *had* died. Damned thoughts started to enter his mind. He had read about this. The experience of death. Described by those who 'pass', but somehow return to mortality after being resuscitated. They're quite graphic in their descriptions – but he was 'feeling' it now too. He was in the first throws of death. The light was getting brighter. The euphoria felt like a huge, great smile upon his own face. He must be dead. He never smiled alive. Brighter still the light came. And yet as bright as it was becoming, it wasn't dazzling. Why *would* it be? He was dead. He had no mortal sight. Brighter and brighter. He began to feel the warmth from the light. He felt his consciousness rise. He had left the shell of his personification and was rising. The light was beautiful. Beckoning him further still toward more light.

He was unsure if he was moving toward the light, or if the light was moving toward him. There was no sense of scale. No sense of depth. It was impossible to fathom. He didn't *want* to work it out - even if he was able – and he wasn't. The light grew brighter still, until there was no sense of beginning or end. He felt a compulsion to press ahead. To move toward. No god-like figure was appearing from behind the light. Maybe this was the moment of judgement? A mortal lifetime of actions. A series of situations born from free will choice. Now being judged. Reviewed. He felt himself at this point breathing out. His last breath? He was here. He really had died. Fuckin' hell.
The warmth from the light got warmer. And warmer. And warmer. It was beginning to feel hot. Too hot. Uncomfortably hot. He felt himself begin to fall. At that point of the realisation, any euphoria rapidly disappeared, as if sucked out by some great satanic force - and through the light, breaking the illusion of peace, appeared a huge demonic face – pushing from behind the veil of light to reveal itself, forcing its features toward where he imagined his face to be. As the demon showed no sense of slowing, the only way to try to avoid it - was to instinctively pull backwards. So, he did.

He jolted up in bed.

The room was fused in a low natural light. Enough to distinguish some of its features. He was at home. It was another morning. He became conscious of his heart racing in his chest, and the subsequent pulse in the temple on one side of his head. He felt nauseous. He felt alive. He felt for his cigarettes.

146

He went to the back door. Slowly replaying the dream back through a mind's projector. He lit a cigarette and appreciated that first hit of nicotine. 'There is often more truth revealed within the reality of dreaming than within this reality itself', he thought – as he blew a series of smoke rings into the morning light, he became aware of his headache. No surprise when you've got ZoZo as an alarm clock. He finished the last of his cigarette before flicking it upward and toward the grass. Before it hit the ground, he had time for another thought. 'Those things *really* are going to kill me'. As he shut the door behind him, the few remains of his cigarette's tobacco glowed slowly to their own death.

He'd given up on writing a book. He'd given up on keeping his Journal. Words are simply words. The world has moved on. Where he was once busy writing, he could actually be busy 'doing' something, something much more practical. He hadn't worked out just what that 'something' was – but there was time. There was always time. It's infinite.

He hadn't been seeing his Counsellor. He'd had enough of people. Their ways. Their words. He had learned a long time ago that the word given to a person like him was a 'misanthrope'.
'a person who dislikes humankind and avoids human society'. Yep, that's where he was at right now. He remembered too some of the synonyms for a 'misanthrope'. Words like 'cynic', 'grouch', 'recluse', 'sceptic' and, one synonymous phrase, 'a hater of mankind'. That was a bit *too* far. Bukowski summed it up (as always). 'It's not that I dislike people – I just feel better when they're not around'. He felt better when *most* people were not around – but that didn't make him a bad person. He loved everyone. Good or Bad. Many of the things that are bad for you - can feel good. Some of the things that are good for you - can feel bad. The universal paradoxes of life.

147

It was the first time that his demon had revealed itself in the way that it did. It was becoming fearful. It knows that it's becoming weaker. All he can do – is give it love and light. It can sense a mortal's fear - and that's what feeds any demon. Fear. Nothing more. Nothing less. He felt that he was tormenting his beast, as much as his beast had once tormented him. The irony. If he was, then it wouldn't be the last time that it would reveal itself. There is nothing spiritually positive about tormenting your demons. What does that make *you*?

The sun was low in the sky but from a certain angle you could see it inside the water from the canal bridge. He remembered the first day that he had moved here. The signets had now noticeably grown and were losing their marbling colours of infancy. There was a pure sense of peace in watching the swans. In observing any wildlife. The ducklings had each developed a direction of their own, spread across the full width of the waterway. Each one seemingly oblivious to the other, until a passing pedestrian stopped to offer one a small piece of bread from a clear bag. Instinctively the rest gravitated toward the food. Reforming into a collective of one. The swans ignored the bread. They appeared more preoccupied with him, standing upon the bridge. The 'grouch' lighting up a cigarette.

Across the bridge was a narrow path that ran at a right angle from the waterway. There was no fingerpost, so he was unsure if the path was 'public'. It looked like it had been walked along, so he decided to follow it. As much out of having time-to-kill than any genuine sense of intrigue. He hadn't noticed the opening there before, and as he walked along its seemingly natural pathway between two bush-lined borders, he felt a giddy sense of childlike adventure.

There was nothing spectacular about the pathway. It was forged through a gentle hillside and it was apparent that with every few steps he was elevating himself, albeit inch-by-inch.

It led into a wooded area, where due to its shading, the air felt colder than the already cool open air beyond its trees. It had the sense of enchantment. The low sunlight breaking through the semi-bare branches; the autumnal leaves looking like gold coins hanging by threads upon Christmas trees. He imagined Hansel and Gretel, scurrying through the wood somewhere in the distance. He stopped. Standing still, he listened.

He was listening for the voices. Any words from the trees. He did this as a child – and way back then – he had heard them whispering.

Silence. Too silent. He had heard that silence before.

Part IV

27

He was here again. He hadn't arrived empty handed. He was carrying a Rucksack. He was carrying his words. 'Cards on the table time'. He baulked at the cliché.

The room felt peaceful. He sat in his chair. It wasn't just *his* chair, but it might as well have been. Comfortable – but not too comfy. In fact, after an hour or so, it started to exaggerate its innate sense of 'lack of enduring comfort'.
'That's life right there', he thought.
He sat down and waited. It was one minute before midday.
'Good morning, sorry I'm late'. He wasn't late. He was bang on time. He pulled out a series of papers before arranging some of them across a small desk to the right of where he sat.
'Right - '
'I've brought some writing with me. Like you asked - '
'Excellent. Was it a love story I asked you to write?'
'It was, yeah. Though to be frank, I'm not very good at love stories. I'm more poetic than a story. Poetry is much more concise. Why write thousands of words when a hundred can show the same thing?'
'Absolutely...'
I leaned across and placed my poetry onto his desk. It was all there. Every single poem I'd ever written, committed to paper or set down in type – with only one or two exceptions.
'How long has it taken you to write all these?' He over emphasised the word 'all'.
'A lifetime'.
'Wow'.

I wasn't sure if he was being sarcastic. It sounded like he was. He thumbed through the pages before stopping at a page. I watched his face as he appeared to read that page. Judging by the number of pages he had left to thumb through, I imagined he would be reading, 'Sleeping' or 'I Suppose'. They were once two of my favourites.

'I'll look forward to reading the rest of these at some point'. He nodded in the direction of the file as he pushed it to one side. It was just me and him now.

'You haven't been here for a while?'

'No - '

'Any particular reason -?'

'I've just felt strong enough to not need the support – and sometimes I feel I often only come here to massage an ego - '

'Whose?'

He was on that too quickly.

'Mine, of course… and sometimes I feel too that my mind instead of 'dumping' trauma, attracts additional negative influences by coming here…'

'Really. Can you elaborate further?'

'Sometimes, when I come here to speak with you, I feel intimidated. I feel exposed. I feel weak. I feel vulnerable. I just over feel. If that makes any sense? I guess if it doesn't to you – then who will it?' I tried to lighten the mood. I could feel it getting tense.

'I appreciate that it can be extremely demanding on individuals – but there is a process that we follow that does facilitate a healing of the mind.' He over emphasised the word 'demanding'.

'I understand that. I think I do anyway. That's the issue though isn't it – I over think things.'

'We're all guilty of over thinking things-'

'Even saying the word 'guilty' implies that 'over thinking' is a bad thing, does it not? I don't subscribe to the notion of 'deep thinking'. That suggests there are levels of thinking. I don't believe there are – I just think we're only just beginning *to* think – and our thoughts too are restricted by many things – not least language. Paradoxically, when we marvel at a genuine sense of beauty or bewilderment, we're often 'lost for words'. There are *no* words that can describe the true notion of the Creator. If there are – it's yet another distortion from the truth. The truth simply *is* - '.

He must be getting fed up with all my nonsense, this guy.

'I understand what you're saying. I have my faith too.'

He must have seen my eyebrows rise slightly.

'Of course I do. Nothing I've heard you say over the last few months I can dispute. It's a very abstract notion. God. The Creator. Spirituality. Many of these concepts are arbitrary to each individual. Have you ever felt like taking your own life?'

Wow. Where did that come from? That's not in the manual of cognitive dissonance.

'Several times.'

'Recently?'

'Very.'

'How far in the mental structuring did you get?'

'Beyond that -'

'Can you explain further - ?'

'I could but it's past now. It was a dark day. A dark night actually - '

'You do know there is help when things get to that point- '

'Really?' It was my turn to sound flippant. 'Like there's help when you're on benefits. Like there's help with 'accommodation' 'food' 'surviving'. Bullshit. It's a game. On more than one occasion I could have been swept into the seas, if it wasn't for a handful of extremely special friends. They were my net. Not 'help' from a government that plays lip service to the notion of welfare and assistance. The gaps are too great. The fissures for people with nothing 'other' than mental health are too wide and too many through which to fall. It's a nonsense. So too people's attitude toward those with a mental illness. Those illnesses are intangible. People are conditioned into only believing what they can see or experience with the five senses. I can see the irony in that too!'

He signalled with his forefinger to the book of poetry.

'Will I find any answers in here?'

'If you know how to look, then you'll find *all* the answers.'

'Then I'll look forward to reading them.'

He checked his watch.

'Yes, I'm sure you will. You may even find *the* question.'

The chair was feeling uncomfortable. It was showing me it was time to leave. I stared directly toward him and couldn't resist giving him a knowing wink as I left. I'd been there five minutes.

I went to the bathroom – it was straight facing the Interviewer's room. Swilled my face with cold water as I stared at myself in the mirror. Even I could see it. It wasn't a case of what was there – it was more the case of what wasn't there. There was no light behind my eyes – or if there was, I simply couldn't see it. Either way – it had gone.

We both entered the corridor at the same time. He stared at me and after a pause signalled with his eyes inviting me back into the office. I walked back in. I apologised.

'Don't worry about it.' He sounded sincere.

'No, I am genuinely sorry. It's been too long me feeling like this. I know I need assistance. I can't do this alone. It's exhausting. Literally exhausting. Two minutes ago, I didn't have the energy to listen - let alone speak. I've just seen myself in the mirror and I can't see any life behind my eyes. Whatever it is that's eating away at me – it's feasting right now, and it's starting on the last thing in Pandora's box. Help me. Please.'

As those words left my mouth, I realised just how desperate I sounded. How literally desperate I *was*.

He must have sensed my sudden change in mood. My energies had shifted. As quickly as that. We took up the positions we had been sitting in a few minutes earlier.

'I think what may be of benefit to you will be some form of regressive hypnosis - '

'You know how I feel about that - '

'I think that your biggest issue is rooted in the distant past. It's a knot buried so deep that you're afraid to expose what it has become – so you're leaving it buried. Better to rot than reveal?'

'That makes some sense – but no. I know what the issue is – it isn't buried anymore. It's learning how to manage, how to deal with it. That's what I struggle with.'

'Can you share it with me?'

'No, not yet – actually, that's not true. I'm sharing it in there-'

I signalled to his bag – which I assumed now contained my poetry and some of my writing as his desk was empty.

'I guess it's all in there – most of it anyway. It's not literal – few things I say are – but it's in there. You just need to go potholing through the poetry – the musings. Life is a labyrinth after all.'

'Life doesn't have to be like that, you know.'

'Do you know what – I've finally realised that. I'm through the maze but as I'm only just through – I'm covered in life's residues – and some of them aren't pleasant smelling or tasting. I guess even being here is my idea of showering it all off. Part of the cleansing process. Ironically, feeling cleansed brings with it a whole new ballgame. Another series of challenges. Sometimes that's daunting – sometimes it's empowering. The level has risen. The vibration has changed. The frequency. Whatever you want to call it. It's a beautiful thing.' I'd not seen him with a pen. He didn't appear to be writing anything down.

'I know you said you're reluctant to accept labels. However, how do you feel about your 'Borderline Personality Disorder'. The BPD diagnosis?'

'I'm just grateful that I have one.'

'A diagnosis?'

'A personality. Disordered – but in there somewhere.'

And still no pen. No scribble. Nothing.

28

Once home the Interviewer placed down the bag containing the poetry, the writings and the musings on the kitchen table-top. He remembered thinking how heavy the paper felt inside his bag, and if this was in any way connected with the gravity of the words printed onto the papers? Of course it wasn't. That was ridiculous. He'd been doing this too long. He was determined to read all that was written. Like he heard, 'it's in there – you just need to go potholing through the poetry, the writings….' He loved a challenge – and this client was challenging – albeit in a familiar, predictable sort of way.

29

Reflections

A paddle steamer leaves the quayside
of a conscious,
filled with the anonymous faces
of infidelities.
None of them can afford a smile.
Few wave goodbye
or fail to see the man at the quayside
who put them there.
Disappearing along a river of betrayal
leaving just a long shadow
walking away from
a setting sun.

A Friend Once Died

Best friends over thirty years ago
inside a world made from sticks and
newspapers. Smoking the first cigarette
larger than those shaking fingers and laughing
at smoky blue rings that grew from nothing
except small lips and perseverance.
Eating chips and poking shit with sticks
and the pets kept inside matchboxes.
Lighting blue plastic and staring at the wonders
of smoke and dripping fire
and all this
in a lifetime one afternoon.

Before a Father told someone,
you couldn't come out
that those Saturdays would have to change.
We never played in the dark.

'Too young' never seems right
when spoken from the mouth of a child
but he was. Too young
to see the bouncing ball of adolescence
breaking windows and hearts
and making sense of a single day
that lasted all summer.
Climbing trees that were once beanstalks
which have long since disappeared

under asphalt carpets
leaving just a giant
hiding inside the clouds and
within them a cherub smile
and for a moment I know it's you.

Now the sounds of over 30 years
are pushing a go-kart filled with laughter
and on a chilled hand where scars remain
a smile from a man who was
allowed to grow older.

Waving back up to the heavens
and toward the boy
clouds separating each
of their smiles.

Words Have a Wonderful Voice

You fry your words
like sausages in a pan
then leave them tied to lamp posts
like hostages under the glare
of a poetic torch.
We have ways of making you talk!
And the words tell everything
they sing and whistle like the birds
finches and parakeets with colours more vivid.
And whether the feathers of grammar
cause a tickle in a throat?
I tell you - let the words sing.

Oxford Road

Thousands of faces
from which hang
angry clothes
that tell a world
what it already knows.
Not a single smile
just a melody
of melancholy played
through buds which
drift into the forest of youth
and a wood
of the working man.
Chewing gum stars
on pavements
shining brightest
at night and every
lightest thought is
carried with the sirens
and a flash of city blue.

And the rain frowns
complaining that it works
too hard in this city.
Landing on a thousand
faces like tears.

Stains

With the vulnerability of cigarette ash
falling on white flannel trousers.
I sit still.
Thinking of the consequence
of the next few seconds
and any decisions made in haste.
Then it occurs to me that it doesn't really matter.
Not to me anyway.
So I blow.
After which an imperfect stain
spoils the perfection
but not the trousers.
I sit still.
Thinking of the consequence
of the last few years.

It's real - surrealism

A good friend keeps goldfish
inside the headlights of her car.
Feeding them at nighttime with
flakes of halogen.

She drives in her sleep
and only last week
she saw a sugar puff
rob a man made of Elastoplast.
'It was awful' she exclaimed
but nonetheless
informed the police about
what she thought she saw.

He looked like a sugar puff.
They didn't understand
those hairy police.

In a milky confusion an identification
masquerade was arranged and she was
face to face with a cereal box.
'But they all look the same'
was her woeful sigh.

Similar, my dear, similar.
Like those goldfish
swimming inside your head
lights.

You left

After you left, I hardly slept.
But when I did
the sleep from my eyes
was just as stubborn.
With nothing to do with time
I planted this sleep
into a ceramic pot
and waited until it flowered.
Not surprisingly it took its time
but eventually I saw the shoots
and with them I cried again
like when I grew spring onions.
And instead of you
sharing our home
I have what looks like a turnip.
Like for like - as they say.

Now the sleep is gone
And in its place sit tears of joy.
Shall I water root vegetables
with all those tears?
If you must
I hear you say.
Madness shakes me by the hand.

After you left
I hardly slept.

There's the Door.

It was those eyes.
Fettered by cliché
no words would
challenge their beauty.

It was those lips.
Their lingering taste
still with me now
as always.

It was those breasts.
And how you groaned
and smiled a pleasured
smile.

It was those thighs.
Smooth and tasting
Just like those perfect lips.

It was that heart.
And how you
gave it to a deserving man.

It was those toes.
Crooked
and hairy.

You had to go.

Awake

The smell of Sunday arrives.
It plays squash inside the nostrils
and the fear of being awake begins.

Watch them as they wave goodbye to dreams
the soft furnishings of thought
destroyed by
that bastard consciousness.

A Photo

Black trousers hang inside a robe.
They share an unlit space with
worn woollen socks
and nothing much more except
photographs inside a
red shoe box.

On days that choose themselves
and when the light finds its way
inside. A father walks
back into a life.
Filling the holes
with his worn pictures.

The Big Smoke

A blanket of bank notes fell onto my city
together with a dust of war.
Layer upon layer soaked into the red brick wall.
Filling the hole of decay mined by
neglectful men who carried their smiles inside
a briefcase. And when I walk through my city with a
sun, a layer upon layer of smiling people
with shopping bags and hats filled with debt
remain anonymous.

Sitting alongside the Duke of Wellington,
two neglected men laughing as they listen on
telephones.
A newspaper inside each open attaché.
As the wheel of fortune
turns in empty silence.

Police Find Body

Behind splintered doors and hardwood frames
lies a silence choked by a mess of thought.
A stillness borne of a confused and troubled mind,
the glint of light casting a shadow aims
its shade at fatality.

A whisper in silence caught
by an acute ear familiar with what it will find.
Untimely cessation. Real and putrefied.

The fettered thoughts of youth and its reason
lie in silence now unaware of its finality.
A quietness sacrificed for a second - forever.
A tortured soul now free leaving tears
that fall on doubt and regret and love
siblings and parents provide grief and remorse.
Blue strangers wearing their big hats
standing dignified.

Love is nothing but an egg.

I was a raw egg when I first fell in love
dropped from a height no bigger than betrayal.
And I watch from the ground
as my hard-boiled friends fall
again and again.

Inspected in their boxes for hairs
and fissures.

Poetic Paupers

I build my poems with words.
Letters gathered from language like a
road sweeper would our chip papers
rolling through streets of thought.
Then curse as slimy nouns cling
to familiar verbs like gum
on a blackboard of asphalt.
Rhyming couplets too large for
this machine sit motionless in shadowed
doorways stinking of piss
drinking with their spellcheck mates.

Those rotary brushes don't care,
gathering the 'gentle' and 'cellar'
with the 'twat' and the 'curly'.
Digested into a stomach of reason
and rhythm or assonance rhyme.

They become words later spilled
onto a pile of other words with
vagrants and crows picking for
gilt edge tat like, 'humpty' and 'dumpty'
to get them through their day.

In the evening while birds sleep
walk the poets with their trowels,
metal detectors;

reflecting.
Where they will stay
and rummage
until a warm sun of achievement
fills their pockets.

Beware

When the deep voice of despair
whispers inside your mind.
When its voice
flirts with the angels those
fading cherubs of light
and persuades them
to have one last
bare knuckle fight.

Beware of death
as it rides in the saddle of fear
racing together with time.
Neck and neck.
When the voice of reason
whispers inside your mind.
When its voice
strokes the hair
and kisses those red flaming lips
and denies them
this one last chance.

Beware of infidelity
as it rides in yachts of regret
racing side by side with ego
encouraged by anonymous faces.
When the sweet voice of rhyme
tickles the hairs on a soft nape
and remembering the one last time

when despair and infidelity, a state
when all those voices were too loud
that they never made any sense.

Beware of the silence.
as it makes its way before you.
Racing together with sympathetic
applauds and the deep voice of despair
clears its ugly throat...

Beware of vacant expressions
of puzzled looks and furrowed brows.
Beware of hairy palms and stripy cows
and little Policemen with bushy eyebrows.
Beware of talking pages
if they really do talk.
And boots that were made for walking
if they really do walk.
Beware of pregnant women
or lifesaving swimming
in your pyjamas,
Holidays won to the Bahama's.
Politicians.
Used tissues.
Beware of being too aware.
A paradox yes.
Beware holy socks
And dripping cocks
Rings and knocks
Shags and fucks.
Beware.

Tupperware.
Beware.
Couldn't care.
Beware.
Nearly there.
Beware.
Be wary
Be hairy
Be smooth.
Be good.
Be gentle.
Beware the deep voice
of understanding.

Beware of Jimmy Krankie.
Confusion personified.
Personified confusion.
Confusion in a box.
Confusion to end all confusion.
The mother of all confusion.
Confusion from a bottle.
Confusion in a pub.

City Rats

It was the eve of a solstice
a reason to remember the rain
and its natural menace.
Guided away by a city's gutters
past a vagrant and the church
toward the unseen sewers.
A veneered stream over bitumen
a riverbank, its kerbstone
seeping water where water never
flowed before the solstice.

As minutes ate away at dusk
the bully rain relented
leaving a serrated cloud through
which milk white light shone
a pointed light.
Lying in the artery of a street
a reason to remember the rain
and its natural menace.
A child lay unconscious
battered by children
who fled like salmon
the opposite way.

Passing a vagrant and the
church.

It was only a wall.

As the cold war began to thaw
during the winter months
of snow and beer nearly
twenty years ago.

As the Berlin wall burst its banks
and a river of unfashionable coats
flowed through the heart of my television
prompting a question 'will I get home for
Christmas?'
Those scarves like driftwood and
flared trousers sailed past
and a huge moustache
filled the screen of my television
with nothing but hair and sounds of excitement.
'Freedom!' Someone shouted, perhaps
one of the bearded ladies with legs
like hoover bags, it was hard to tell
in a foam of laughing faces.
Overhead 300 kilometres away
I hear our freedom.

The Royal Air Force with its concrete arsenal,
its water pistols of peace held at the temples
of people who wear odd socks and sing in the sleet in
temperatures of minus 13
with purple faces
steaming great gouts of exclamation

into western air.

And I realised then.
There is nothing unfashionable
about freedom.

Nan.

Will you pull a cracker?
In your mind you turn
to see the face of over 80 yuletide seasons.
A tooth now stained with port wine and
above which dangled a faint moustache
of Irish stout.

Hair thinning taking time
before every smile
and those ears of
a thousand costume diamantes
reluctant to hear beyond the distance
of her loving arms.

Inside the lady burned a
fire of irony with flames of resignation.
Waiting to turn her corner
before she went.
Leaving all her life inside
a miniature pack of playing cards
won from a box of
luxury crackers.

Trains

Today I saw them on a train
reading about yesterday.
Tomorrow I'll see them on a train
reading about today.

Routine fails to write anything
worth reading about now.

Playing the spoons at Christmas

For three hours that same day
from tea to sherry
silence to smiling with
children who relished the difference
between the minutes.

Magical, musical spoons held
inside hands that toiled and fought
for these moments.
This little time always spoken of fondly
throughout the years.

Now Great Grandchildren
eat their jelly
with his instruments.

The Art of Being Late

An alarm clock has two functions in its inanimate life.
It alarms and it clocks the seconds that eat into the
three score and ten of averageness.
Occasionally, after surges of intangible currant
it flashes or waves at me from across a bedroom.
Telling lies.
This accelerates my metabolism
but slows any rational thought of the simple things.
Like how I regain full consciousness or
simply - how do I dress my foot in a sock with holes?
Through a lens of clear glass
a window into a world of shapes doesn't disappoint
with its stray dog shaking and shitting and double
decker buses filled with blow up dolls and children,
uniformity in the unruly slapping of each other.
And traffic that I wouldn't usually see
and a wife dreaming of work.

Vitruvian lollipop people.
The personified warning gauge for my tank of time.
Sadist bastards standing in my hasty road to
redemption grinning with their anonymous faces. And
every child who ever walked to school, leopard
crawling placing more seconds of my time into their
day-glow lunch boxes.
Bastards!
And every Give Way giving way to strings of traffic
a love bead of heavy goods followed by their smoking

entrails filling my day with metaphorical cloud.
And those sneering satanic red traffic lights
as far as my glazed eyes can see
and, Oh my God!
A triangle of information.
What should be a man digging with a spade
turns into men wearing lime coloured jackets
drinking tea.
Standing over the hole of reason
for the surge in time
and its clock.

Semantic Dispute

Today I dress myself in soup
with scotch broth brogues
laced with linguine.

Then I drive in my car
made with self-raising yeast
through the Mersey oven.

In Birkenhead I find myself
raised above the rest.
Looking at empty shelves
where once gingerbread men
worked, turning marzipan
into ships. Before setting
sail into a porridge of uncertainty.

And the confusion lent by
semantic dockers as they strike
for fear of working. Conditions
abused by a management of punctuation
and exclamation!
You see?

Temper

I finally found it.
Hiding in a shoe box
underneath our bed
where it must have
fled after those hurtful
words that we spat.

Now that we're
reconciled I promise
I will never lose it again.
I'll bury it in the garden
with our old dead cat or
that lazy tortoise.

Wait. There's no bloody
room. In the garage or
in the bin perhaps?
Under here? Or maybe there?
Bollocks – that's full.
Have you seen where I can
put this?
Silence.
Do you know where this goes!?
'Do you know where
I can fuckin' put this!!?'
Too late – fuckin' lost it again.

Her

Her name will never leave me.
It hides in the trees
or the autumnal leaves
each one a smile
that fell through the sky
effortlessly.

Her voice will never leave me.
It sits on the breeze or inside
my mind
playing her piano.

Police – 'Metrolink is not a playground'.

A welder's flash from worn steel is
caught by the impatient eye that
squints to follow the arrowhead
and its level of mercury track.
The linear landscape
its regular stillness and a haze
from boiler filled noon's that
marry nature with graffiti red walls.

'Sir Matt Busby' arriving to ignorance
following its routine of day
leaving with a rhythmic clack
and silent laughing children
walking nowhere the opposite way
against a motion and hissing brake.

Starlings standing overhead on
their trapeze - a furrowed brow
showing silently – 'how or why?'
watching the birds as they sing.

Coloured platforms, a stage
to shout, to run, to fall, to scream
and later a wreath of condolence
will pale with the memories.
The anonymous starlings fly away
carried on the screams of youth.

Police Race Against the Clock

Time insists on taking us all for fools,
it lends itself whether we
wish for it or ignore its consequence.
Then it appears in minutes that feel like days
as years in love are gifted as minutes.

An equal share is never the same.
Squandered or cherished,
rarely appreciated – when it is
you leave, often too early.
Seldom too late.
It's time you fool.

Mad Man

Yesterday I heard a fly talk
I kid you not - a fly talk.
A talking fly.

Later that same day
I heard a dog laugh
I kid you not - a dog laugh.
A laughing dog.

Later still that same day
I heard a bird sigh
I kid you not - a bird sigh.
A sighing bird.

Just before the end of that same day
I heard a gunshot.
I kid you not - a gun shot.
A shooting gun.

Today I saw a man die
I kid you not - a man die.
A dying man.

Ram Raid

Standing looking toward the glass a
transparent division of social class
separates the few that have into the
many who don't and never will.

Fuck You! The labels sneer with
figures too distant as children live
with the concept of cannot afford
seeing their reflections in a T.V

Mother's comfort with an arm
a grin and a display of open palms
as their Mothers' showed them how.
Reflections in a window becoming smaller,
whisperings of 'tomorrow', 'next week',
'not today'.
Between a sigh and the tomorrows
under the sheet of city dark
cars crash through the reflective division.
A four wheel down payment
with its own label.
Fuck Me? Fuck You.

Olivia

You have never looked into my eyes
or held a thought about what you see.
You have not heard the voice that
gave you your smile and your tears.
You refuse to hold the hand
that failed to guide you in its darkest time.

Yet would you want to look into my eyes
and allow me to hold my thoughts?
Would you want to listen to a voice
or let it tell you how beautiful you are?

The silence forces me to imagine
the beauty of your soul.
The stillness demands my silent prayer
through which I hear you,
I smell you; I touch your face.
We smile together
and in those almond shaped eyes
I see your pain
and wonder how forgiving words
will ever pass those perfect lips?

Wasted Day

I have waited a lifetime for today.
Now that it is here, I ignore it.
Like I do the sitting man
holding a dog
or playing two notes
on a flute.

A Memorable Day

Every day that passes
is an act in a talent show.
Each waiting patiently
one behind the other
called to life's stage by
time.

Some days cannot
sing or dance, standing
in line queuing patiently
behind or in front of the days
that we will never forget.
The days that shock. The
days that will make us cry.
The days that will bring life
or take life as they tap
dance or play piano.

A star performance
by nine eleven
and in the wings and the
shadows, unseen and
unheard - the day we die.
Waiting to be dazzled
by the light.

Heroes

Through a cataract of net curtain
he is staring.
Entombed within brick and age
the struggle of a fading mind.
On the dark mantle rests a sepia past
inside veteran gilt-edged frames,

over which hangs an image
a graduating face
inside the flowered wall,
watching over a parent with
a two-dimensional concern.

The rhythm of a beating clock
the countdown to a turning page.
Answers to the questions
left rotting inside a home.

Outside Policemen walk
and all is well with a world.

Weekend Ends (Part I)

Ankle deep in the aftermath
of a town's festival of litter.
Watching girls dressed in
Primarni frocks walking home to babysitters
feasting on greasy meat and
cliché compliments from the man
walking with her to a bed that glitters
in the darkness they call weekend.
Intimate moments spent upside down
inside a house filled with toys.
Nothing more expected from a town
where its people shop inside catalogue
aisles of debt and its men and boys
are fed on a diet of Rugby League
and bravado and intercourse with
women who they know but have never
met until last night.

Inside the sounds of reality brought with
the morning stew and sobriety
he flees leaving somebody else to take
their turn inside the soiled sheets
where an innocent heart will break
over time and repetition
of hollow words.

(PART II)

A labouring diesel engine stands idle outside
the unfamiliar house that smells of children
and deceit. Pictures of cherub faces smiling wide
with missing teeth quicken a pace to a run
down a garden path strewn with dog shit
and the familiarity of last night's papers.

Inside a head the pain of imaginary staplers
forcing alibis and stories between the ready
mix of daylight and its dull grey sky.
A driver asking too many questions
offering hope and fantastical suggestions
of where the night was when he
chose to be anonymous before
coming inside her and in between his dreams.

An empty house with its familiar smell
and pictures of cherub faces
smiling wide with few missing teeth next to a
picture of two perfect smiles.

(Part III)

The sound of abuse echoes from the street downstairs
through curtains made of nylon she glares at what is
now her past
behind exhaust smoke.
Staring at the empty bed she sees herself in the night
her eyes squinting with the reality of empty bottles
and half smoked cigarettes wearing her lipstick.
Inside the bathroom a tap dripping into a sink
resonating its metaphor for her life
as she saw it. Trying to escape with the men she would
flush down toilets.

If she had a choice.

He Died Too Late

To a child it looked like he was alive
for when he smiled
he would expose his perfect teeth.
And when he laughed
they would fall from his mouth
into a handkerchief
lay out in his lap.

Sitting all day in clothes
that always remained the same.
Hiding a consequence of battle
that diluted a life thereafter and
made a father's father lame.

Through mature eyes and history
which told of the Somme and
the 1st Regiment
Seaforth Highlanders
and a young private
a Mother's son.
Standing proud in colours and braid
those sepia ceremonial boots
filled with huge feet
and a responsibility,
before a great war
had stolen handsome looks
but never a determination to stand proud
and salute a sovereign crown.

And the pictures that are played with
inside any mind could never begin to understand
or imagine just what went before.
To see him sitting in his chair.
through a child's eyes misted in youth
to see an old man sitting in his chair
whose own tired eyes
would stare toward a child.

Who would see those thin red lines inside
squinting grey orbs
and only years later
would he begin to understand
the horrors carried inside one man.

After his war where others had died
in fields filled with acrid smoke and tears
and screams of friends
his brothers in arms
crawling into a hell
pieces of them
landing by his side
steaming gouts of fear
to mask his own pain which
began that same today.

Loss of life or limb
and the beginning of a suffering
that would eat away inside him

over months, over years.

Enduring every kind of hardship
including guilt and every vivid
moment re-lived inside a sitting room.

In Novembers since
standing tall and walking
like all men should.
Shoulder to shoulder to salute those
whose blood was spilled into fields afar.

Tears were never shed
laying wreath after wreath.
Before a return to a life
that we all knew
as peace.

Cardboard Spaceships

Empty cardboard boxes were my cars and spaceships
and speedboats and houses and sanctuary.
Filled with darkness and eight years of imagination
my world always smelt of new corrugation.
Like everything in a life, it was left to those vicious
elements to soften the resolve of a cardboard will.
Watching as my spaceship wilted in the garden
peppered with intergalactic meteorites falling as rain.
Houston. We have a problem.
And Ma' a new fridge freezer.

Didn't We Have a Christmas Last Year?

A day as grey as fish and
a Tuesday without pancakes
wraps itself around my soul.
As the yuletide arms
extend and welcome me
I struggle to avoid the image
of long telescopic arms.
The end of which - a handshake.
Merry Christmas
Is it really? I think.
Merry Christmas to you too. I say.
At the end people are filled
with toys and pickles.
A silence.
Some would call it a glow.
Others - drunkenness.
The finality of unconsciousness.
And a Happy New Year to you.
And you too. I say.
Before driving into the drizzle
of next year's Christmas.

Time & Distance

The hatred is still with them.
Behind occasional smiles
a residue on every spoken word.
Holding hands with the moon
before they embrace.
Patience smiles her beautiful smile.
It's been so long since I heard your
heartbeat. In silent days and darkness
I listen. Through the years of emptiness
I hear it.

And the hatred snarls
like a fettered dog would.
A Mother's face sneering
back at a Father's.
Time and distance
spinning their webs of deceit and lies.
The hatred is still there.
It always will be.

Craig the Snake

I have a pet snake.
His name is Craig.
He isn't slimy like
some folk think.
He eats crickets
yet I've never seen him drink.
How fucking strange.

The Cornish day

A ruffled patchwork quilt of fields
with their fraying gilt edges,
tempt a steady ocean and offer cattle
the chance to stand motionless and
stare into the minutes that
yearn to fill a lazy day.

Those fingerprints left by hazy
stratus on a glass of snow globe sky,
fail to halt the style of this clear day
revealing in minute detail
the blurred edges of our city world.

As the evening's lamp is shone
reflected by a menacing surf
a world of silent beauty allows
a glimpse at our insignificance
and the future that remains
upon this still earth.

Mr John King

Wrapped in the hours that seep through time
allows for thought of your destruction.
To poison the unspent hour that sits
waiting under the shaded branch of reason.
And when revenge comes. He will be swift.

James, gifting footprints on black sand
where a drunken stability is built.
Those simple traits of inadequacy
raining still in your dead soul.

This makes no sense to anyone
except to him and those who know.

A Picture of Nan

On the grass that never grows
under a tree that never weeps
a gentle mouth that never speaks
rest the hands that touched my face.

In the shade that will always be
on a day that will never change
with smiling eyes that never cry
rests the women who we called Nan.

The End

The reality of sobriety
for the man who doesn't taste
wine or women -
just every word
of every song
in all the books.

The Angry Frenetic of Phonetics, Love and Television.

Last night on the Bravo Bravo Charlie
I watched Romeo and Juliet
and realised then that I hadn't read Bill's book
about the story of young love and yet
I felt more than qualified to spit at the Tango Victor
such is my distaste for love and the mess that it drips
onto pictures of loneliness that some refer to as
bachelorhood.

If I should choose to involve myself
with love and casual Sierra Echo X-ray
then some may say that I would never be understood
because I utter phonetic riddles and make it hard for
my lovers to inch ever closer to me.
Bravo Oscar Lima Lima Oscar Charlie Kilo Sierra
I say to all of them.
And still they don't understand
They're idiots - do I have to spell it out for them?
Hope Our Love Lasts And Never Dies.
As hard as I try - that is far too bold a statement.
I could lament about what happens when you become
hairier than me?
Can't you see
you Tango Whiskey Alpha Tango.
Phonetics and love just don't mix.
Am I a poetic philistine?
No I am not.

Will I be your Valentine?
No I will not!
Now Foxtrot Uniform Charlie Kilo
Oscar Foxtrot Foxtrot.

'cos Romeo, Romeo
Juliet Bravo's on the Tango Victor tonight
and with love and tele - there are no choices.
cos after that
it's only fools
and horses.

Sharing a bed
with words and dreams.

The coldness fills an empty bed
and pillows show where
troubled minds once lay side by side.

Now words sit on a rising chest
a conduit to another world a
sailboat of superlatives in
a sea of thought.
Those words hold a hand and guide
through oceans towards a faraway
land and then they leave.

A jungle of imaginative fear,
vipers and spiders and
lizards crawling over time
and its consequences.
Loneliness filling holes left
by deceit and the darkness
waiting for those that
stand and point and watch.
The horrors that were without words
to steer the sailboat through the
storm of dreams.

Images forged through life
and its wickedness.

Leaving no alternative
but the reality of words
that now rest on a heaving heart
and read through
dilated eyes.

You said - I said

Holding each other in our arms -
we stared toward the darkness -
or the evening sky
as you preferred to call it.
But with hindsight - darkness was staring me in the
face - it was so, so obvious.

Back then -
we were gazing at a salvation.
Look - a shooting star!
and we made that one wish
and kissed under a moon
a moon with its pasty face.
I swore she looked surprised
that old girl luna -
where men had once raced
to pull down her eyelids I said.
Old crater cheeks you said and
I should have known then.

The following day I read that
an International Space Station
was visible to a naked eye.
Imagine how foolish I felt.
Making a wish upon an artificial star
or that bus in the sky filled with boiler suits and beards.
You're no Russell Grant you said
I 'm not am I I said

Thinking - just what would Aristotle
make of Russell fuckin' Grant in his
bottle green jumpers and
I should have known then.

And when I kissed you
as you climbed aboard that merry go round
at the seaside
and I saw you disappear
inside a black acrid smoke
and that bloke with the panic in his face
carried you from
an gilt painted horse -
and children were crying simply because
a Victorian gearbox had seized.
I told you it was old You said
Industrial heritage I said
apologising with little sincerity and
In a roundabout way -
I should have known then.
And when you asked

Does my bum look big in this?
And the answer was wrapped in acidic wit
with a bow of bright red truth.
Your bum looks big in anything.
And you laughed.
You laughed so hard that you cried.
Those first real tears.

Don't cry I said

Why not? You said -
and I couldn't answer and
I should have known then.

And a Father shaking a limp hand -
forcing all the circulation into a
party popper celebration of
engagement and drunkenness
and a mother in law
I know what I saw
She didn't you said
She did I said and
I should have known then

Then those golden rings side by side
the size of a bagel
and a spaghetti hoop.
And I wasn't able to get it
on a finger and that singer
in the choir
that you called a minger
but I just knew her as Grandma.
Well I've never met her you said
because she lives in Edinburgh, I said
and I should have known then.

And what you found funny
never made me smile.

And I would belly laugh
at a man wearing a stupid fez

and you said that anything he says is not funny -
Who says? I said.
I say you said.
And the words grew into serpents that spat and poured
twisted venom
over the years that we'd spent together -
And whether we admit it or not -
that's when we fell out of love.
Just like that - I knew then.

And now I see you inside my words
like you're hiding inside a wardrobe and
waiting to scare the darkness from me.
It's absurd just like when you said you were leaving
and you went
but said nothing.
Just leaving your spaghetti hoop on the kitchen table
but taking one great big bottom with you inside those
trousers.
If only we could wish like
we could disagree
I said - to myself.
Before throwing my golden bagel
into a darkness and toward old crater face
into what was once an evening sky.

Then - there in the constellation of irony

I saw it -
a shooting - bastard - star
Too late I said
I know whispered insanity.
Never Too Quiet for Silence.

Walk with silence by your side
and watch as it paints its pictures
with pastels of imagination
inside a mind.

Listen to silence at your side
and hear as it shows you everything
you want to say.

English

I look forward to English
like I would a warm bath.
I sponge myself with words and wallow
in the suds of lexicology.
Once the vocabulary has cleansed my mind
leaving nothing but occasional letters,
I allow these to fall down the plug hole
into the semantic sewer, to swim
with the numbers
and the rats
where they belong.

Locket

Why bury the hurt inside
with charlatan smiles?

Painted with pixels
a keepsake will whisper its lies
for generations. Until people
they stop caring.

Replaced with smiles
of their own.

A friend called 'Dead'

A man I knew called himself 'Dead'.
and he said that the irony was that
one day people would call me by his name
and not other more foolish names.
What scares me is -
he was always right.

Grown Up

Remembering those days filled
with heat and sticklebacks,
wearing spawn as mittens
and snake belts that hissed
in the face of fashion.

Faces brushed with soil
and stained with tears
as our heroes
are ordered inside
by those Generals wearing
heated rollers.

Evenings
where the sun would sit and talk
leaving just an orange bedside lamp
for the moon to read her stories.
Until those cheerful eyes began to fade
along with a child's words and thoughts.
Adolescence standing in the shadows
with an impatient father
who they still call
'growing older'.

Zaminashuns

Every thought and theory learned
placed into storage jars
left sitting on a shelf inside a mind
that's filled with other things
like the Karma Sutra
and Wednesday's game.

Just to sit behind a desk
with ninety minutes in which to
weigh out the contents of those jars
that now look so alike.

And every answer is nearly there
playing swing ball with recollection
and in the end, they sit back down
and kick off their shoes,
smoke a cigarette, pour a beer
and when they're ready, then maybe,
they'll open a door
allowing enlightenment
to leave his mark.

Poetic Jungle

Inspiration wore a camouflage jacket
and hid amongst the trees.
Coming ready or not shouted writer's block
searching with binoculars and HB's
poised at the ready.

And inside the concrete jungle
hide those graceful metaphors, hunted for their
qualities by a man wearing
idioms on his feet and a heart on a sleeve.

And those Gazelles gathered in herds of words
a superlative jumping the highest, and adjectives
smelling of the greens and the browns.
And in the distance feeding on leaves of
imagination
the baboon with its huge hairy bottom
or was it the humble writer
chewing on a rhyme
that was simply forgotten.

My City

My city smells like any other.
A sewer runs under its streets
over which walk the people
carrying debt and infidelities
inside grey minds
and telephones.

My city looks like any other.
Its murdered sons buried inside wood
over which walk the people
carrying flowers and uncertainty
inside soiled hearts
and sawn-off shotguns.

My city feels like any other.
The police and the sobbing mother
tell me so.

Seductive

When our eyes meet
I undress you.
I want to part you and insert
my thoughts inside you.

I want you to tell
me what all this means?
I hear 'tempting
or attractive things'.
Still, you have inside you
too many 'E's' like that
sister of yours
'seductively'
but it's hard not to be
turned on by both of you.

3-minute philosophy

The world is so complex is allows
mankind to fight wars and make love
at the same time and debate the irony.

Many fight love and make wars.
It is only history that teaches us nothing,
the future which tells us more about
what we aspire and the present which
allows us to consolidate our emotion.
And that, as they say, is all there is left
but more?

And the egg did boil.

Counting holes in crumpets

There is much to read
in John Ryland's bowels
it's just that a world on wheels
and hasty limbs
care not for enlightenment
but a cultured emptiness
which fouls our towns with
celebrity and girls in films
who boast their tits are bigger
than the towns where we live.

There is much to read
between those lines
at a BBC
their linguist ponders
on rhetoric and things
that they think
we will never understand
like wars and things innit.

And the girls read our forecast
for the umpteenth time
leaving Gordon to wallow
in his verbal slime
about 'Eric from Staybridge'
growing a root vegetable

bigger than ours
in the same breath that briefly
mentions a war
somewhere or a conflict
or whatever it became.

And while all this occurs around us
there are those that take the time
to count the holes in their crumpets.

The Rain Stays Away

We were friends once.
Before our clothes were strewn
inside rooms with their miniature bars
and afterward we would stare
at the outside where
you always wondered 'why'
about the stars
between the moonlit clouds.

Whereas I wanted to know
how long it would be before the raindrop
would separate
as it ran along the outside of a window?

As I think about those days
I wonder if you ever found the answer
to your questions –
or me, the question for all your
other answers?

Mr Amazing Misumgooma

Apart from his name he was anything but.
He'd have his dreads trimmed once a year
listened to Bob Marley and drank Red Stripe beer.
His words. Not mine.
So what have you got to say Mr Misumgooma?
Well sooner or later I'm gonna meet my maker
so I'll just keep practicing what I'm gonna say to
him - or her.
His words. Not mine.

Well start by explaining how you crashed into a wall
and killed two people who'd done fuck all. My
words. Not his.
He licked his lips and cleared his throat.
Well if they're dead then I'll not need mi coat.
And I'll live my life inside this cage with the rage of
demons that I'd been feeling - until today. Cos the
men that I killed killed my son. An eye for an eye -
or so they say.

I pained me to feel what I was feeling
but Mr Misumgooma was truly amazing.

Be Aware of Bettaware

I never expected to see him in my lifetime
but yesterday the Devil came to my house
under the guise that he was distributing
Bettaware catalogues.

The money isn't great but it gets me out the house
were his exact words and before I could tell him I
didn't want a giant slipper or Tupperware dishes;
he fixed his gaze into my eyes and I saw my soul
burning inside his pyre of damnation.

You'd better come in I mumbled
before chastising my dog for snarling
and salivating loose threads of fear.
It's only the Devil I reminder her
and the Devil did smile
like only he could before patting a dog's head
one last time.

And as he sat I could smell my life
inside his clothes
and I began to wonder just what he knows about
my life and how he found out where I lived or if the
word forgive was contained inside his catalogue?
So I asked.

Do you do forgiveness?
I do but it comes at a price

and you haven't got that much money.
I know by the way you've lived your life
there is nothing in here you can afford.
He showed me the catalogue
and I'm sure it said 'Redemption'
and with that we began to walk
toward darkness.

Leaving a dog to sniff at a me
that moments earlier had laughed
at the thought of a giant slipper -
one on each foot.

Wilf

They gathered outside a widow's home
uncles and brothers and grieving sons
smoking cigarettes with no sense of shame.
Exhaling bending flutes of smoke
into a morning filled with modest silence,
broken only by the hum of a jet engine
and
everyone looked toward the heavens.

Then he arrived, behind immaculate glass
and the eyes of working class women
began to fill with grief and the sobbing
of a son could be heard by neighbours
standing at their doorsteps just as he always would
on such a day when the sun failed to shine.

Comrades paid their respects
with their time and the relevance of glinting medals
and people behaved like everybody expected
in a way where nobody ever feels comfortable.

Peering through the dividing curtain from light into
dark a sense of mortality carried on a breeze that
fluttered those polyester suits and pleated skirts and
those that gathered took one step forward.
'Ashes to ashes - dust to dust.'

Now women stare

down at their enamel chipped toenails
and it goes without saying that he was loved
and that he will lie
in a resting peace.

The cry of wood pigeons
whispers of goodbye
a last tear from a son
before a final wave
from a wife wearing ebony shoes.

A Family and Their Sun

It hides behind Tupperware cloud
having warmed the soils
for a squinting dog, a cat
the one with the twitching nostrils
on the other side of the dry, wooden fence.

Occasionally we see its strength
changing frowns into smiles as it wraps its rays
around the smells of our burgers
who spit their flavour into an afternoon
where work
is sitting downwind away from us all.

And everyone drinks to make
everybody else that bit more interesting
talking about varicose veins and
hairless legs with inexplicable lumps.

I think about the burgers
and those bald sausages,
tortured over white hot coals
hissing their resistance
Oh, how they got off so lightly.
Leaving me with just the music
of beginning rain and a voice
We're leaving now.

Domestic Violets

She remains with her hands inside water
as tepid as her dreams.
Through a mist of window she stares
toward her autumn
and it seems that
her life is standing still,
unlike the clothes on her washing line.
They dance like her soul would dance
if it hadn't been beaten.

Whilst inside are the flowers
staring apologies to
the pictures of children.

And she realised then
that she couldn't last
another summer.

Church in the Sunday Night Rain

A grey morning
rolls over and scratches its ass
as God clears away
half-filled glasses from days
that are quickly forgotten.

Tattered starlings look pained
like we all would standing in a puddle
up to our bare skinny ankles
competing for worms
that don't barely exist.

The blackest crows' overhead
fighting to be the first
to fly to church, to sit and squawk
over a priest's dull words,
sitting on what's left of a lead roof.
Proof at least
that one commandment
is ignored.

Sitting on aged oak with squints of discomfort
are a congregation in its loosest sense.
Spread out in isolation, mumbling for forgiveness,
gifting loose change
arranging their memorials
like they would furniture
inside their heads.

A simple cemetery like
a mouth filled with broken teeth
and underneath lie the people
who would wish that they could
see at least
one more Sunday in the rain.
Even if it does nothing
but itch its own ass
and drive the bearded fellows' insane.

Songs of praise bellow from
two dimensional Christians
for their fleeting moment of fame,
before we hop with a remote
sense of religion
using soap to cleanse our souls.

Hurt

Making love for hours
is familiar to these hands
for they stroke for your pleasure
and insert themselves into an intimacy
of unchartered love
filled with myth and legend.

We can pretend
that love has hoisted us
upon her shoulders,
turned colder than faucets etched in blue
that stream their contents from unknown origins.

Yet, it was only a kiss
forged from lying lips
where words now mean nothing,
they just soil that cloak of purity
into which you blow your smoke and warm
yourself.
Hanging by a thread of sanity
from those gallows
of abuse and disappointment.

Yes, if apology was allowed into your world
he would wear soft shoes and walk
inside every room of your mind
whispering simply, 'I'm sorry'.

Maybe the bitterness on which you tread
would soil magic carpets
of contentment,
leaving a sunrise to warm the wings
of butterflies,
those beautiful colours
of your thoughts.

RISE

New

no love withers
in its own silence
gestation through
long dark seasons
before
light
and then
the petrichor.

Chat Up

He would stare
and listen
as she tied seven colours
into seven knots
with just her words
or the way in which
she looked into those eyes
as
she fed each hue
with just a flick of Thursday hair
or a smile
and watched him swallow
each and every syllable
into the resonance of an empty heart
and
as those colours
flowed through dead chambers
he felt the rainbow's arc
and once they reached a soul
he only ever felt rain
and sunshine
elements
that one day
he would taste
and love,
love and taste.

Star

She could without even trying
hold a star in the palm of her hand
and with just a touch more imagination
she would sew the cloth of her darkness
into the whole of every night sky
seamlessly
folding it back toward a daylight
before anyone would even notice
except the stars
the nine muses
and me.

The Value of Meaning

During the humdrum
of random flirting conversations
she felt the need to say 'I simply adore cats'
words that scratched for a moment at an idiolect
'so you're an Ailurophile', I said
with a certain amount of satisfaction
that time spent eating dictionaries
had not been wasted.
'Don't be so rude' she hissed
diluting the worth
of a first in Media
while showing me that certain chatoyant quality
of her beautiful, beautiful eyes.

Sleeping

I never did tell you
in that moment now dissolved
how much I would cherish the heat of our mornings,
how I wanted to trace the letters of a Greek alphabet
with the skill of a tongue's quill into intimate depths
of arousal and your blood.

How I would watch you sleep,
imagining death your allies, your lovers,
untouchable tomorrows

and I never did tell you
in that moment now among time's own healing
how I would whisper the names of ancient Grecian
towns Roman gods and Philosophers
while touching the freedom inside your hair
or how I would sense each day of your life's longing
the hurt and pain of rotting love
reluctantly worn around
a heart
a wrist
and the bone of an ankle.

I never did tell you
for just that searched for single moment
when darkness concealed its reasoned limit
how I wanted to gift you the emptiness
of religion's ultimate destiny
and how you would wait a short while

standing next to your chosen devil

gathering those pieces
of love's impatience
until that perfect morning
when I will follow you there.

Kissing Inside a Cathedral

Walking
hand in hand
respectfully of course
one wearing bright coloured clothes
the other content
with the threadbare sounds
of well-worn unfashionable words
they stopped,
standing
upon the decks of autumn's night-time shadows
in amongst the bones of wealthy men
and the tired trees of families,
silently
reading from the font of chiselled Garamond -
later
much, much later
inside and away from the dark of
previous days
beneath a splendid ceiling of faith
a kiss from silent lips
in tune to the resonance of a symphony
filling the fissure
between her knowledge
and his words.

First

Remember that first night when we fucked
after the others where we could but didn't
and we both knew then how it looked
how nothing would ever be the same again

not in this life
or the next.

Empty

He realised as always
much, much too late
that a summer spent reading
the likes of Collins or Bukowski
did nothing for a heaving miserable soul
except highlight the futility
of pouring the heat of cheap spirit
into an already empty man.

Final Word

I often imagine those last few words I shall utter
while hanging in a position
deemed too uncomfortable for dying
with the weight of my old bones
and sodden liver
later resting on whorls of worn springs
and not a Priest or a Vicar in sight.

Not quite as often
I imagine the last word I will write
like at this moment,
tracing the swirl of a very, very last letter.

Ideally, I want it to have a French origin
or Greek
or I'd settle for some little unknown noun
with its root in Sanskrit
but not, no, never Latin

while Scandinavian 'loans' I always felt,
sound much too harsh
undeserving almost
to be read above the silence of a Coroner's Court
to people who will never quite comprehend.

Last Night

During an evening spent without shoes
and smoking duty-paid cigarettes
I offered my conscience a handsome chair
just so that we could sit a while
or as long as it would take
or as much as we could tolerate
listening to the words of each other
without feeling tearful and ugly
and so it sat with me
listening to the haunting of Gregorian chants
and staring at the reflections
of over three hundred days -
we spoke about pathetic hair
how loneliness appeared to follow it everywhere
and why opinions are often simply quotes
taken from hand-me-down books
we smiled and bounced the odd generous brow
in that exaggerated mock-disbelief regarding stuff
and we charged our glass into the silence that followed
accepting that
there are stones for every pair
of life's comfortable shoes
then
we spoke about the oceans
and how they've become
a cellophane of see-through clichés
the dull lids of winter skies
and how they look like Tupperware
about Bukowski and Oscar and even greater men

we imagined and spoke about
riding the bare backs
of two white Camarillos
before walking through
the resonance of Northern Galleries
containing Waterhouse, Rossetti
and Millais

we inhaled the detail of expression
from a memory of The Lady of Shallot
and we knew from its existence
that there had to be a sacrifice
on which to fasten a streaming ribbon of fate –

so as the morning bled through sores of indulgence
and a conscience bowed its dutiful head
pressing itself into the flesh of a hapless lap
the sight of love it shone once more
through the seam of two lifetimes
and toward
the beating sound of
existence.

Calling Time

Head down
reading the collected works of another
and contained within its worth
the poem Are you drinking?
sits alongside rats of difficult choices
left to forage
among what remains of her.
I think that I am just ill with life
is one phrase that I recall
and it plays to the tune of sadness
the only sound worth listening to
during every Monday afternoon –

despair
disguised with
a mask of laughter
where lost souls are tilting their life's failings
from glasses stained with destruction
into haggard, lavender flavoured
grins -
time to stop?
Time ladies and gentlemen.
Time.

The Wood

They lay between
the shade of the cheeks of two trees
within the green blankets of its ferns
purple buttons of its flowers
and they stared
at the stillness in one another
inhaling the scents from a single June Saturday
hours inside a bowl of memories
gathered from a gorgeous, gorgeous wood.

The two trees stood either side of a man and a woman
four hundred years of knowing in their leaves
and they whispered to the silent people
they will cherish one another
and the flowers
through mouths perfumed with colour
chatted with dashes of dragonflies
who all appeared to have agreed
they have begun to love each other here
she,
counting the joys and the sorrows
on the shell of a Ladybird
and he,
with the weight of two buttercups
in the palm of a hand
realising
this is an example of perfection
a beautiful place to die.

The Hill

It's now
as the gilt disc of today
rises
and three starlings
sparkle because of his stares
their breath
never seen throughout winter
can now be heard
above the sound of loss -
white dots of mutton
pressed into pages of hillside
dark cattle
for each mistake?
Oak trees
the backs of curious heads
gathered
at the hilltop
to observe
in shocked silence
the darkest ever wave
in the distance.

Gone

Yesterday
perhaps the day before
or the hundreds that existed
in between,
I read the words
drink from the well
of your self
and begin again
those words
wore no heart
on the sleeve of any sound
no wide-brim hats of superlative
nor carried with them flowers
or playful smiles -
instead
they simply gathered together
as if sitting for a family photograph
sunshine in their faces,
and the profundity of their meaning
became slowly visible
inside every pair of
squinting,
weary eyes.

I Suppose

I suppose, I suppose, I suppose
we could lie here naked
share our heat with the purr of two selfish cats
and stare at those tiny flecks of intrigue
into histories of each other's disappointments?

I suppose, I suppose
we could whisper our favourite words
wrapped inside the aching
of each and every breath
and stare - and stare as we share the delights
of anticipation's scent?

I suppose we could simply hold each other
with the strength that only weakness allows
and stroke the very flesh of our uncertainties
and touch - and touch till that sense of what's missing
is there beneath the tips of silent fingers?

I suppose I could simply say I need you
in that way you must have seen a thousand times
and let you watch once more
as those words
destroy me.

Flame

She bought him a cigarette lighter
had it inscribed with words of his own
he rediscovered it
inside the pocket of a casual jacket
between red silk, slightly torn –

he went to light another cigarette
inside a room he now calls home
but it failed to spark
or ignite or slowly burn,
the irony wasn't lost
in its turn.

Weekend

She lives nowhere
and everywhere she dwells is beautiful
until Fridays and Saturdays
or love.

She walks outside
and everywhere she steps is wonderful
until Fridays and Saturdays
or love.

She talks frankly
and everything she speaks is melody
until Fridays and Saturdays
or love.

She loves honestly
and everything she loves is indestructible
until Fridays and Saturdays
or love.

Sorry

The tips of my fingers are numb
with cold and pain
through years spent smoking life
drinking
from upside down bottles
loving
with a love I couldn't afford
to give
at an age
described as
'the youth of old age'
'the old age of youth'
take your pick.

It feels inadequate
to type the words 'forgive me'
knowing that she is sleeping
let alone
while she's awake.

Moon

Today
or this morning
to move ever closer to exactness
I read another love poem
written by anonymous
and contained within its form
those poetic shows of awareness.
I found myself more than disappointed
to see that the moon was, once more
looking melancholic
as it were
staring into our sad, sad history...
where
it somehow shared our photographs
and to reinforce this slender personification
looking beyond a lost love's horizon.
All I could see was a falsehood
like the 'Moon landings'
but, arguably,
more elaborate.

Other People

They all possess their opinion
which they treat as if it were
their own child.

Defending it
with all that they are
and all that they will have
and ever be.

I say
quite casually
'no, thank you'
which is often confused
with arrogance,
whereas 'allow your child to grow
and in the space that they leave behind
teach yourself to think that perhaps nothing
is like it appears to be'
which
is much more profound
don't you think?

Post Coital

Last Sunday
wearing just a wristwatch
and
a precious stone between the two of us
whilst
underneath the distant sirens and the church bells -
we spoke of the things
that occupy our heads occasionally
and I recalled during moments like this
and with varying degrees of fondness and regret
that the rest of our lives would not be wasted
so, after fucking
we lay as if practicing for death
me
still and staring
beneath the coastline of an island paradise
in that old water stain on a ceiling
you
thinking about the people
who you'd really like to fuck?

As We Slept

we wore the Andaman sea as our shoes
planted the roots of candles in the sand
waited until dusk threw its blanket around us
so we could wear the stars as hope
and the moon as a hat,
yet we never did dance
with those flickers of hip jiving shadows
we chose to sit
with the old man Jack instead

and all too soon his stories became tiresome and weary
(we'd both heard them many, many times)
before the tide took its care to remove itself
taking with it the soles of our shoes
as those golden fingers of morning removed our hat
whileJack crept away with the stars
as we slept.

Tell Me Bad Things

I beat you
slapped you 'till you dropped
to a floor
allowed
the air from this dark room
to be part of me
forced
the heat from my fingers
to be part of you
gripped
by a necklace of hands
to be one.

Punch & Moody

The man secreted behind the horizon
pulls at the string of the white-hot balloon.
That's the way to do it!

I want to see the silhouettes
of a huge wooden alligator,
a hooked nosed protagonist
that string of sausages castings shadows
into feet standing in an audience of sea froth
and sunset surf.

Instead I see a half disc moon
hiding inside a thumb nail
as a pinch of beach prompts too much thought.

Just the stars and infinity
watching the foolish man thirty miles from home
walking in the footprints
of an ass.

Standing with the Gods I

Gazing at the might of Amphitrite
in all her stillness, her colours, her taste
it is never beyond a mortal to imagine
sailing her serenity, riding the ringlets of her waves
her tides and great storms
but to survive this unforgiving ocean of insincerity
into which softly spoken words were often poured
he must stand at the feet of Poseidon
and observe for the rest of his days
the expression of yet another God
at what can never be tamed
unlike the nature of the horses
simply,
alone amongst the Gods to swallow
those salts of doubt and suspicion
that the earth will ever shake again.

Standing with the Gods II

Your life is myths and legends
your sleep is peace between your wars
and for a time, I stood between the two
for a moment,
in the moment
recalling too a myth of the fox of Teumessian,
a Cadmean Vixen
its cunning and your guile,
your curse keeping on
and me, perhaps the nemesis Laelaps
a paradox for the Gods
who decide on this occasion
to turn simply hearts into stone.

Standing with the Gods III

comfort them Apollo
comfort each and every thought in their day
shoulder the Nyx of night-time too
watching Venus, Aphrodite
and all the other Gods they could share
dancing with contentment, blissful thoughts of future

comfort them Lunar
take the might from the swords of their words
dilute them with your tranquillity
comfort them Mother with the stories of your rivers
your trees
and your woods

comfort her, comfort him
comfort them Thanatos
in your warmest darkest blanket.

Standing with the Gods IV

Erebus stains her heart with a kiss,
promises of greater existence
drying as they hang in the burn of Hemera still,
she fears Chronos
making her mere mortal
standing silently amongst eleven of life's twelve Titans
waiting for Eos to open heaven's gates
upon that perfect, final day.

One

Until the folds in your pillow look like mountains
and the warmth in your bed feels like snow
until the air that you breathe tastes like yesterday
and the sounds that you hear are in **bold,**
until the blood running through the bone of your fingers
taste less or more than four simple syllables
or the sky is grey with the weight of regret.

Until the peace that's expected is betrayal
and the oceans and churches are no longer with us
we are.

How to Kill a Man Before He Dies

bite the teeth of your lies into the flesh of his sincerity
trace the shape of your heart into his palm
wear a silver brooch of his voice around your neck's
nape
let your hair fall onto the face of his insecurities
build cities with promises and speak of few regrets
walk with him into the surf of green seas
listen to the breath of his sigh in the flow of perfection
ride on the sandstone backs of chiselled lions
sit in the glow of seven Egyptian sunsets
and simply smile
laugh and giggle as you come,
as you come again
feel the heat through his eyes
and stare into each of the battles that he lost
recognise the few that he won
and then
love another.

Light

had this idea for a poem
but it isn't really a poem
just, I guess, arguably poetic
n' shit
but spent around thirty minutes
this morning
talking and laughing
with Niaomi
who
some say
is special
autistic
and fourteen
I remember thinking
any person who can make me
and my black dog laugh
right now
are much more than special
they are
light.

The Irony of a Final Word

so, you now grip the heat from another
no stranger to your golden breath
or the honey from your cunt
but, will he ever see the mischief inside those legs,
that freedom inside that hair now fettered to a guilt
or just a single star?

survival is never noble when standing at the side of love
just as worship will come in its many, many guises
words will now not be one of them
and every indelible word written will become rotting
cathedrals the congregation of their meaning losing faith
with what was true and what was not

survival is never noble when standing at the side of love
read the same page again and again
read the same page again and again
read the same page again and again
madness shakes me by the hand;
it feels limp-wristed and is not as tall
or as poetic as I'd imagined -
disappointment is an understatement.

Hey look, here's the sunlight
fuck, that feels hot
am I in some kinda hell
have I been in some kinda' hell?

survival is never noble when standing at the side of love
and why does a refrain keep insisting on playing its small
part?

Who
What
Why
Where
When
How
?

after what you said the other day
about just needing to know -
it now all makes so much sense
I don't want or need to be forgiven
I'll simply see you back
in those days and nights of hell.

Porphyria's Lover Boy

I saw them both they were awake
it happened not like they did spake
Porthyria his love did not glide in
for she was dragged about the chin
screaming and cursing at her love
with her passion and her lust
who smacked her face a neat three times
until she fell to midnight chimes
and as she lay in motion still
his lips did lick at was this thrill
from his pocket he did produce
a length of cord tied as a noose
around the silks of perfect neck
he wrapped her death but did not check
where she could hang, and he could see
where she would sway from mortality
with all the might of her own lies
he raised her bones into moonlight
which shone onto now naked flesh
through clear blue glass of diamond lead
and fettered her legs so wide apart
tearing lace in flickers of light
she gasped at air from his spoken breath
but did not scream it has to be said
he entered her with fingers raw
and teased her spirit from its soul
and as they squirmed at the end of rope
she gained no fear and lost no hope

he pushed his blade inside what remained
leaving love's stillness and one heart stained
he lift her down and lay with grace
and stroked an anguish from her face
and in the silence that comes with love
he pierced his heart just like he should
to lay beside her forever's day
and no god spoke, even I have to say.

Tonight

the sky is liquorice black
its stars are simply stars
its air as cold as it's over

but there was a time
when we poked our joined fingers
into the chest of a great bear

and it roared in its own delight
and our moon, our beautiful friend of a moon
wasn't there to see it.

Friend

I have this old friend
although I'm reluctant to call them
a best friend
simply because if I do
I 'd feel that life had already beaten me
but
they have told me things straight
saved my life on more than one occasion
ate my food, drank my drink
even watched me sleep; getting high
and low
and the lowest
yet
today we sat and watched that man
that writer, that poet
and all this friend saw was 'a drunken old man'
and
all I wanted to say was 'you just don't get it'
but
I already knew that my old friend did.

No More

since you left
I have again kissed the forehead of Nefertiti
dipped the fragile bone of a finger
into the steel of a biblical river
and stared once more at the despair in Mengin's art
and the eyes of two children -
I have touched the stone of a minster
and walked through streets in counted footsteps
stared into the dark secrets of autumnal clouds
read books and decided that
some writers are much more than gods;
Fante's Arturo Bandini said
'what got me were her eyes: their brilliance, their
animalism
and their recklessness'
and I wept
I have weighed the values of loneliness and alone
and spoke with women and men of equal worth
smiled at ravens and heard the laughter in their wings
spoke to the sons of religion and seen a madness in their
beards and wept again
I have ravished the flesh of your worth
and tasted the importance of existence
broken more than one sunrise with my thoughts
drank the blood from the vein of temperance
and will weep no more,
will weep no more
will weep
no more.

Two Days in York

as a boy before the mortal sinning
I remember touching the blue iron of The Mallard
and climbing into the dead lungs of steam engines
of golds, purples, greens and blues
and smells of sulphur aboard an unkempt head
the minster was a biscuit coloured beanstalk
wisps of clouds for its leaves
they moved at their chosen pace;
muffled bells spoke more melodic than any priest
if that was ever possible?
we would stand in lines to queue
to witness
god's own
house -
apparently,
even
then
you
could
ask
him
for
forgiveness
as a man after much more sinning
I remember how much smaller the beanstalk looked

how I could step over it on my way through another
almighty day
I felt like Lemuel Gulliver
maybe next time I could take it home
and bring with it
god
and those muffled, musical bells
to use as little gifts like earrings
but, I imagine
that would be stealing
and god would be a long, long way from home.

Pain

Today
unlike yesterday
it is falling
with the weight of snowflakes,
silent unpredictable weight
tomorrow
it will be something else
love, almost.

Four Horses

Standing
with purple hands
furled inside pockets of shallow denim
waiting
for today's serpent of a train
I'm
taken by a stillness
in the air I share and breathe with
the mute of commuter
and there is an old man
who appears as if he has lived
a hundred more lives than any one of mine
standing here just out of reach
in pain it seems
he smiles apologetically
senses my melancholy
then stares back into the silence
of distance
eventually a train, our train
arrives
one of its headlights is broken
and we both embark
side by side
him choosing to sit facing me
before staring through a window
our window, travelling backwards
so that
I notice just before him
the four steaming chestnut mares
standing side by side

in their own great green universe
and I notice that their eyes
seem to gaze into our window,
following our moment.

He smiles again
the smile you give to a stranger
when you know they're slowly dying
and all I can say is
'what beautiful horses'
and he nods
a tired and weary looking head
ever so slightly
and replies
'yes, they really are'.

I Want You to Fuck Me (Performance Poem)

a lady walked over to him
she had hair that you'd only ever see in the movies n'
a smile you get to see just once ev'ry hundred dreams

her voice was a late summer evening n'
her eyes would break a heart into a thousand stories
before she leaned right in n' whispered...
'I want you to fuck me for as long
and as hard
as you possibly can'.

as you can imagine he was taken aback
by the gravity of her words and their meaning n'
they caught him unguarded and ill prepared
'lady, you're a few pages ahead of the women
I've loved before n' you're racing to the end
of mortality's story
but if you really want me to fuck you
for as long and as hard as I possibly can
then I think it only right you should know this.

I've been fuckin' women for as long and as hard as I can
for as long and as hard as I can remember
but I'm getting older and remembering is getting harder
and shorter than the member that was once longer and
harder .
You look confused - here, take this glass...
Lady, I ain't gonna fuck you or love you
but if you wanna sit in the skin of that wing-backed chair
I'll explain, just let me say this...'

now I watched all this as a third person
as this man regaled the tale of his story
she laughed and she frowned
giggled and gasped
and raised her brows as he explained his craft
before finally she said
'and just how long have you been a writer'
I heard him explain
'being a writer
doesn't apply to
every situation'
before she was howling to tales of masturbation
and how this was married to the state of a nation,
politicians and bearded women

'enough - enough' she demanded
'instead of fucking me for as long and as hard as you
possibly can - will you just write about it
and exaggerate it - like writers do - and all men?'
'Sure' I heard him say.

She stared at him with dragon green eyes
and smiled a smile that said
'I want you to fuck me
for as long and as hard
as you possibly can.'
That's right baby, for as long and as hard as he can
and for as long and as hard as he writes

I.N.R.I

It usually lasted around an hour
a lifetime in every single week
(two hours or infinity at Easter and Christmas)
standing
sitting
kneeling
a short walk for bread
and absolution, apparently
miming at least three unknown hymns
one rather melodic when sang
in that waste of time Latin
or it could have been English
but never Welsh
 under our irreparable roof -
curling throbbing toes
inside a discomfort known as Sunday shoes;
sweet smells from indoor clouds
the odd bell
offering not giving
deep stained unbroken glass
and huge 'fuck off' (bless me father)
hardly ever lit candles
staring at the twelve stages
of the cross
in particular the one where Jesus
a man with a misshaped beard
died or was sacrificed or summat
outside a lifeboat station
and for even thinking that

a gentle reminder from the softly spoken man
that we will burn for significantly longer
than forever
in a place called hell
or Wigan
as a couldn't give a toss father
would always scoff
before a flock would shake
the right hand of God
as this same divine palm would
pat the unkempt styles on their heads
filled with questions
with a trinity of yellow-stained fingers
and a Nan
with an incredulous tone
'Loifeboat station? Sweet bay-bee Je-sus'
and the raising of a brow
from a woman
wearing an oversized crucifix
much, much too large
at an angle on her busters
for any real show of faith
to be taken seriously
by a boy looking forward
to the pick and mix
and a life without none
of this.

Deadness

deadness will not see
the purple flakes of his sunrise
nor the Raven motioning
in the air of darkest to light

yet it stands upon these sands
beside all the seasons within him
in the grain of his words
and their meaning's demise
so, before another sun will fall
as all great empires and their love
spill out a man's mind
offerings to gods of purest loss

let it swell with each fold of an ocean
effervesce in tide after tide
take with you every promise and its residue
remove everything of value from him
feed what you will to the colourful
fish and the creatures
then watch what in turn
we become.

=

that man said
'do it only when it is burning out of you...',
well, right now, it is burning, like a thousand awkward
souls -
so, here goes...
the heat inside these eyes she will never feel again
not
like he feels the snarling teeth of her lies
forever gnawing at the sacred bones of truth -
days will not always be named after gods
but the cape of her falsehood and the mask of a deceit
will always disguise the temper of the seasons
into one creature -
she may lean against the breast of another
eat their manhood with a relish reserved for a saviour's
feast
and, they may laugh, of course they will laugh
until time
reveals its own hand
until time makes it all
=

Random

We can eat soft cheese
pour fine wine and recall our dreams
turn the pages of this Roget's
deciding if the next level of mortal resonance
is influenced by the profundity of nine six seven
and Brogi
and randomness
or fate?

Flesh & Bone

Smile at flesh and bone
fix the weight of your life
into
another being's consciousness
by staring,
allow them to talk with you
saying nothing
at all
except
goodbye my love
my love, goodbye.

You are God

The fashion in the clouds is predictable
another man has come
over who you will drape your days
and nights
talk to him about what you know
tell him each word you hoard
in that way you breathe the lust of sentiment;
but words are like empty, hollow churches
truth faith of word is blessed
with a congregation of meaning
and
you will always preach to no one
except your own god.

Truth

Let him lay these final words inside this ground,
the bones of a voice that they'll become.
Let the worms eat their truth;
you never did, you never will.
Let him watch as your words absorb into another
the barbs of a voice that they are.
Let every truth of us sit beside you
and share your living days and nights.
Let them all know that what is inside you
is everything but a truth.

Sheol

you have had their breath
their pleasure; their sorrows of lingua
their heat, the warmth of their flesh
their bone
you have had their tears
their delight, their beads of exertion
their salt, the worth of their words
their souls
and in return all you would take
was not quite everything
without leaving Sheol in its place.

Sometimes

time will not scoff or gnaw at this,
arms of distance will never be
force enough
skies will never flake from the loss of this
words of poets will never be the thaw
nor strength enough
breath is no measure or scale of this
softness in nocturnes is never quite
enough
but sometimes, only sometimes,
Sometimes is more, much more
than enough.

How Silent a World Becomes

folded over a knee of dark thoughts;
spanked with
a determined hand of loss
of regret, of knowledge
beating those past days and nights out of us
was our pleasure not our pain,
but just a look from you could be a fist
a question, an elbow in his thoughts
or a kick –
smile for him baby
let him lick and kiss the beautiful face of your cunt
let him enter you harder than anyone
steal your breath and every ecstatic cell;
he will break himself into the smallest pieces,
secrete himself inside this black of space;
between the sincerity of these words
but
you
will die
and I
will die
oh,
how silent a world becomes.

Wear

Wear nothing,
just a favourite heavy belt; you must remember
wear scent
the sweetest 'I have to fuck you' smell
with that pair of handmade earrings
wear loss
a miserable sense of loss; you'll know the one
wear black
your most perfect 'make love to me' colour
the hardest of veneers in which to console yourself
wear death
it looks so beautiful from here, right now
and if you're reading what I'm asking of you
it's late afternoon before a perfect morning.

A Sunrise will not Always Speak a Full Day's Truth

an ocean is not the keep of me, nor a sea my wings
though they shoulder the greatest skies of light and dark
season the hope left to taste in a feast of broken
holy well, oh holy well
talk with me
press the chin of a solemnity moon
into this nape of loneliness
absorb all my darkest days, all my loves, all my failings
as only you can
I know you whisper still amongst the letters of flying
gulls,
and I remember how you bathed an old man
in your tides of gentle reverence, showering him
with his own spirit and drenching the despair of age
in your depth, in your magnitude, in your grace
holy well, oh holy well
stand with me
bear down the colours of your day
upon this canvas of my naked flesh
take from me the oils of a year's darkness
leave me with just the weight of these scars
and the smell of her
and in return
I will gift you back a spirit
for you to use
as a truth inside a sunrise.

Rise

from where I am lay
I am, of course, looking at the stars
and
I can see the letters and the freedom in the black
of flying birds;
you are one of them now
soaring beyond any man's imagination
and if it comforts you, please know
that when I turn
to lay upon a true face of beauty,
into this same earth
I will rise.

Throwing Stones from Silverdale

from a sitting position
he would often throw stones
not real stones
just the type of stones
that you're (perhaps) throwing now,,
stones that loop from one side of a mind
then land in the soft swaying grass of imagery

now the word 'stones' is getting on his tits
and yet 'getting on his tits' doesn't belong here
not here among the pattern of daisies
that remind him of that southern hemisphere
he once saw in a well-thumbed glossy book
filled with stars and galaxies
not here
with the chin of a moon
swilling its hairless face inside the stillness
of a pond
where sheep and cows lay upon blankets
of moonlit shade
shone from the girth of menacing trees,

and that's a frog – not a toad
is sitting content beside the patient pole
of an evening fisherman
willing a child to stroke the green marble
of an amphibian
as a plosive bubble
now sits upon knowledgeable lips.

Children staring back toward a father
for that reassuring dip of a head
before a gentle stroke with the tremble of a finger
with a huge wide-eyed smile that she knew was a simple
realisation that frogs are not nearly
as bad as what a man had once said.

And through the fields
filled with memories and butterflies
he wanted to show them how it was,
how the evening would smell of eight forty-five
how an inch of cigarette
would stream its sweet-smelling smoke along his fingers
how he stared at a profile of Louis Armstrong's lips
sitting upon the grass from a shadow puppet fist
eating flies to the tune of a wonderful world

and as the day lost its way
leaving in its place the inks of yesterday
he writes loops of unnecessary words
and wonders if there will ever be enough
and waits
as they take their turn
to throw stones
to throw stones
to throw stones.

Two Suns

lately, just lately
there are few things
that can compete
with that feeling you get
lay upon the heat
of an otherwise empty bed,
dusk melting
through drawn curtains
into a room
where
a picture of two beautiful children hangs
on a wall;
and they're both smiling
at me
and this life I'm within,
'You Get so Alone at Times
That it Just Makes Sense'
is the latest book of Hank's
that I'm reading
and whatever 'it' is
does begin to make sense
his words fill each kind of emptiness,
the fissure between emotion and truth,
falling effortlessly, fine grain
between stones of a life's many days
filling what I thought was
already full of more words, more light, more hope
for them, for us

yet
I couldn't recall ever having read a poem
about his child, his girl.

All poets will surely write about their children,
leaving the lovers, the whores, the addicts, the fuckers
the cheats, and the drunks alone for a while
so I searched and found
and read
Marina.
majestic, majic
infinite
my little girl is
sun
it begins.
I smiled to myself
and at my own
three
majestic, majic, infinite
suns
who smiled right on back at me -
two with the beauty of life
in the deepest of blue eyes
another
with just that tiniest glint of devilment
they once called *majic*
flashing from the chatoyance of hers
and they may not know it yet
but I'm hoping
one day Hank will share their lives
too.

The Moment

ink will not drip from the sky today
into the gentleness of Holstein cattle,
those great maps of continents that they wear
in this their world, their existence

bronze will not bleed from the ground today
into playfulness of the stag and its doe
running in absolute silence as they stop to stare
in this their world, their existence

love will fall from his heart today
into the beauty of earth and its mother
to remain in the absolute stillness of today
in this his world, his existence.

Love &

these are the words that
made it through the fire
baby,
these are the words that
are not fastened to a noose of addiction,
chains or chaos -
nor have they been whispered licks or
reeds of a voice into folds of pleasure
baby

these are the words
filtered through soils of time,
stones of untruths
baby,
these are the words that
were never given a mortal's chance
baby.
these words are
the other horn on that same bull
baby.

I See You

yesterday
those pyrite bars of time's light
wore away the beauty of mortality
in yet another morning;
evening
became the black of reaper's gown
in just one word and numbers
'Visiting'
(18.30 – 20.00)
this stage, its lights fading,
show-time for the greatest light the gods' possess
to sit upon the hush of walls,
those shapes of pulsing, twitching beds
in wards, on wards
the gods cannot disguise the scents of death
wrapping them inside petals of hope, around thorns of
fear -
we saw her then
plain and sleeping -
for now
her faith is gentle,
her hands almost glass
her face paper white
she heard the voices
(for we are not the angels)

as the glaze of another dream
faded from her powder-blue
I saw what she had seen
for just that briefest moment;
and
as she smiled and spoke our names
I saw those days remaining
disguised as the faintest glint.

In Time

these tears are not the stars
though some say
they are or will be
one day

these tears are not the weight of night
or golds or greens or reds of hours
though some think
they are or will be
one day

these tears are not the oceans
the cathedrals, the music or that river,
the making love, the fucking, the laughter,
the stillness, the pain, the drink,
the first full moon, the last sunset
or a pyre of rotting words,

these tears
will only
and always ever be
simply
her.

Sappho

I went to see her yesterday
hanging like sorrow should hang
still and beautiful
alive with grief.

I wanted to talk with her
step into her sable world
her mind, her heart
yet before I could, I will swear
that she turned her head toward me
challenging me to the coldest gaze of loss
and in that briefest of moments
I saw a glint of golden recognition in those eyes
of deepest hurt
beguiled yet moving closer
I imagined in her grief that she believed
I was Alcaeus
where she would spend her waking moments
gazing and listening for the melody in the dead souls
of poetry's meanings
or sitting upon the breath of each
and every word we spoke
so I could inhale the complication of her beauty,
stroke the weight of burden from her despair
where each of us will perish within our own free will
from the greatest pain of each other's unrequited love
on the sullen, expectant tide.

Seven Three Seven

only last week
I was standing above
a stubborn smudge of cirrus cloud
walking over foils of silent rivers and seas
and before me
the backs of tilted heads, some containing dreams
a body's claim to weariness, others
a life's gathered anxieties and memories,
to my left
a gold leaf of Lago Tresimeno
to my right
the faint spots of Dalmatia
while before me
for just that briefest of moments
was the whole of humanity's
existence
where later
any god or man
could see the yellow punctuation
of their towns and of their villages,
reading the silence of land's black pages
and imagine that it was they
and only they
who created all of this -
this week
I am lying beneath
a blanket of nimbostratus
staring at the long-lost soles

of those few footsteps
I walked as a god.

A Tiger Sunset

In those evenings by a red sea
I would often gaze west
and see the tiger's eye
staring over its den of desert hills
a single life in its predatory stare.

I remember thinking
as those nights each fell away
'it really is a beautiful world'
while sometimes, I would just stare
or make wishes or promises
to all those once cool cats;

as it left for distant cities
it seemed to wink at a man's imagination
but what I couldn't see behind me
was the faint claw of a moon
piercing the huge cage of black
I always thought of as protection;

a tiger is still a tiger
while it sleeps
or when it roars.

Time will Conquer Time

a
weak
light
shines through
a gauze of distance,
time will conquer time, will conquer time
they say
the armies of silence, of missing
are defeating imagination, unknowing
each
the deadliest of swords
where will her love now be,
where will her love
now be?
amongst the touch and the sounds
of fairer weather, the golden voice
of Beltane's promise,
she will become the day,
she
will become
the day;
a nib
of heart
will press down heavily
into the pages which they wrote
together

and the nights that will never be written
will one day begin to bleed
from her
just as they do from him;
time will conquer time, will conquer time
they say.

Rabbit

there is a weathered, stone rabbit
in this garden,
its eyes, fixed on me,
suggest that it's lived a long but
very unreal life -
now I'm wondering
what it would see if it ever looked
into my eyes?

if only I could have kept as still
as the weathered, stone rabbit
that's lived a long
but very unreal
life.

Thunderstorms

a guy
I was talking with
recently
said,
as a child
he collected thunderstorms,
kept them inside glass jars
airtight
and
in the dark -
do you still have them?
I asked.
'The glass jars
or the thunderstorms'?
he replied.
Either
but I'm leaning more
toward the thunderstorms.

Addict

to some it is a beast,
to others that beast is Heracles
fighting reality's twelve labours –
but we once shared the same dark,
slept inside each other's black
hunting our lies and our preys together;
there is always room for yet another shadow
to take their place,
you left with strength and grace
never turn back, back turn never,

there is a garden upon this earth
where its nature is too much for any beast to dwell
so I have to imagine that you are now sitting
in an Eden, Hesperides
or that wood
together with the other nymphs, tasting the colour of
their apples, their memories;
leave me to this world where the beast will torment me
and I will torment the beast
so you can sit for a time
in the light, beneath the sun,
amongst the flowers of truth
and your peace.

Charon

as I lit the day's last cigarette
leaning through a downstairs window
the black slap of night air
was immediately upon my face,
its taste reminded me of another moment
where I leaned from the bow of a merchant ship
cutting its way through an estuary's skin
sounds of sea-froth and empty miles ahead.

I could see the stars above two countries
and with just the turn of a head
a black panther of headland
crouching in the distance.

I imagined I was sailing upon Acheron
and briefly that I was Charon
with a great hold absorbing
all the dead souls,
but that was then
when things were not quite as empty -
tonight
there is no sea nor river on which to sail
just yet another darkness
except for the tiny fish of a cigarette
glowing to its death
and a final breath
of grey.

Cheers

It was by chance
by coincidence
if you believe in that kinda' thing
that I saw a picture of her
holding sunlight inside a Capri glass
filled with tiny fruit
hued with exotic colour,
and she was smiling
with her back towards the sea
a sea she often spoke about

and the moment painted itself
with the blink of another's lens
but what they didn't capture
what they couldn't even hold
was the animal behind her eyes
the sparkle of her love
not even a glint, the tiniest glint of her
as she smiled.

Now

and the green of life has faded
melodies of success a distant tune
 if, and only if, we choose to listen
to dance, to fall.

Generation after generation learn little
dividing chaos into tiny pieces
this world is as grey as silence – let the colour of hope
paint a masterpiece
an exhibition of life after love
there is no crucifix inside these walls
or sitting upon this flesh; every love story
has an ending
and often with just a single word
hello.

First Step

even the Journeymen will still their hands
or their feet for a while,
stare into the arrogance of the tides
their swells of persistence; the solitary sea-bird's
insignificance
and realise there cannot be one without the other –

what allows this moment
for a man made of days and bone
to stare into the silence of time?

and when peace finally finds you
it will sit amongst those words already written
not these that are being bled
or those about to be formed
with the light.

The Bloodiest Battle

the speed of these depths is quickening
darkness slaughters light, butchers hope
dead pools of dead prayers
reflect loss and pain, loneliness gains its strength
from silence,

even the flowers from the seed
choose to turn another way,
while music elopes with every shared melody
leaving in their place
the rabid fangs of consequence –
and where was god or Jesus
that son of a god inside this
his bloodiest battle?

Jesus was loving him
and another 'numbers'
and god was nothing more
than a gentle soothing
from
behind the words.

Part IV

30

He was exhausted. It was the fifth day of the month. To his name he had 3 cigarettes, 4 eggs, half a pint of milk and even less in the way of enthusiasm. Just the thought of that made him reach instinctively for his trilogy of cigarettes. He wasn't eating – so the eggs would remain at 4. He was fasting. It was his second day of a 72 -hour fast. He lit 'The Father' cigarette as he made his way to his flat's back door. There was just enough time to unlock its mechanism before he exhaled the first stream of smoke into the cold fresh air.

The Ash trees were down to their bones. Their fallen leaves curled and discoloured, and well into their journey of rotting and recycling. Nature is ruthless in its beauty. Two starlings were each standing on their own tree branch, they were looking attentive – surveying beyond and away from his own restricted view at ground level. He wondered what they possessed beyond 3 cigarettes and 4 eggs? A breath of wind forced the finger-thick branches to move slightly. The birds didn't flinch. They each just rolled with the motion in their silence. Another life lesson, right there.

He inhaled the last of the cigarette – appreciating its final hit. Reminded himself for the thousandth time that he needed to quit, before flicking the butt into a receptacle at the back door -an oversized plant pot that would eventually need emptying. Soon.

He wasn't hungry. It may have been over 24 hours since he last ate, but he had now conditioned his stomach with these regular 72-hour fasts. He enjoyed their affects. And they were becoming much more frequent. He went to his room to sort through some of his few personal belongings. There were pieces of paper everywhere. A consequence of sifting through some of his poetry and writings before he'd shown them to the 'authorities'. Ok, so the guy wasn't the Gestapo, but he was from the Death Star of Authoritarian bullshit. 'Ingsocesque'. He showed them what they wanted to see. It was old poetry. Old writing. None of which was relevant today. All that stuff was a long time ago. He might as well have shown them pictures of himself when he was a baby – 'yes, that's me, though it bears absolutely no resemblance to the person I am now – but yes, that *is* me'. He wasn't lying. So yeah, read away. Pick the bones from that.

He opened one of his room's bedside drawers and pulled out another file containing papers. This was the stuff they should be reading. This is where the answers lie. It all really *is* – just a ride.

there is a skill to putting on shoes
and taking them off again,
I'd never met anyone
that could do both at the same time
with any real success,

you're either wearing shoes or you ain't
and that's pretty much how people love
in that shallow, uncomfortable way

kick off those synthetic soles
let those toes feel the sun,
that purest love
laid bare.

'Beware the average man, the average woman – for their love is average'. You really have got to love Bukowski – *The Genius of the Crowd*. An all-time favourite. Flicking through the reams of paper revealed many past thoughts. Most jotted down and unintentionally discarded or lost through his inability to see things through to a conclusion. He was convinced he wasn't alone – but everywhere he looked people appeared to be much more in control of their actions. They all appeared to have some sort of plan – no matter how loosely it was held together.

He lay the Journals out before him. Choosing one at random – although he had learned what period of his life the Journals referred to - just by the appearance of their covers. His time spent in Asia was penned into a faded, much handled, A5 Moleskin. It was the only book with a gold coloured tag, inscribed with a message that now read as insincere as it probably was. He reminded himself that the woman who had those words etched wasn't in a great place either – of course he didn't take it personally. We all have our shit going on. That was January 2011. He was lost then too – or rather, he was still 'seeking'.

He thumbed through the Journal – relying on fate to produce a snippet of remembrance …

> 'Last night was beautiful. We set up our 'beach chill' - with candles dug and lit in the sand, a shade and shelter scooped around them and it looked beautiful. We lay there until the candles were extinguished by time alone, listening to the sea and staring at the heavens. We had a drink, but the essence of that moment was more intoxicating than any alcohol, and what occurred was one of those significant

emotional events that will now undoubtably stay with me forever. It became one of those moments you can recall from memory, whenever it's needed, to calm or inspire. It truly reinforced life's fundamental guiding principle - that the simple things are without doubt the most life affirming...'

He remembered that night well. It inspired the poem 'As we Slept'. The truth was distorted there too. He remembered the huge night sky. Its stars. Mesmerised by their magnificence. Their abundance. Their being. Staring into infinity was awesome. He was getting good at it too.

It's all well and good harping on about the past – it helps to give a life some sort of context. What he was beginning to realise, was that the common theme of 'now' – was also there nearly ten years ago. Who was he kidding? It had always been there. From being a child. He just couldn't comprehend what it was back then? He was only just beginning to understand it now.

Every single relationship had led him to this point. Each one a catalyst, each one a recurring lesson until he understood what the meaning was within the lesson. It was really that simple. Upon reflection, throughout many years, he had been an emotional fuck-wit.

His early notion of love was inspired by what he was witnessing around him. Especially as a child. He didn't stop for one minute to seek within himself. Not knowingly – though as the façade began to fall away, the clues had always been there. The signifiers. The revelations. He had just never seen them. They were all hidden in that proverbial 'plain sight'.

He had made a decision. The feeling was overwhelming. He had already lost all motivation to write. His Journals were nothing more than a tangible sound board of yesteryears. He didn't need to know the details of 'why' or 'how' he had ended up where he was right now. He simply needed to deal with the 'now'. He didn't need to write a book. He had too many stories. Too many revelations. Yes, the RAF years were fun. No, he didn't kill anyone. The closest he had come to witnessing death during his time in the Air Force was when he ran over a red squirrel. He might have written about that once. A complete accident. He felt so bad about it that, that he questioned his 'killing instinct' for slotting anyone from a Soviet Red Army. Maybe it was a 'red' thing?!

The Police had challenged him. The deaths. The assaults. The darkest part of human endeavours revealing itself up-close and personal. He never believed people could treat other people in such a negative way – but that was their own free-will choice, to behave in such a way. It was all part of the game. The polarity between the two. Service to self – service to others. Choose your path – and then be the best at that choice. The middle ground is where the averageness seeps through. If you're going to do it – go all the way – otherwise don't even try. The world is full of those who stand in the middle. Fearful of whichever direction they choose. That's what eats them up. Not their lack of ability – their lack of conviction. He had been guilty of that too. Spending a lifetime waiting for it to happen. It isn't going to happen on its own. Obvious to some – oblivious to many.

He checked himself. He often wondered where the pragmatist within him dwelled. It didn't reveal itself often. When it did – it was quite determined. The decision maker. It didn't float about in some whimsical world of abstract thinking. A universe of flowery, quantum entanglement theories and ideas. Deal with the now. Sort the reality as it reveals itself in – the - now. That's all you *can* deal with. Then the 'butterfly effect' will simply do what it does. No more writing Journals. No more writing poetry. There comes a time when a person needs to stop. 'Deal with what you have'. 'Enjoy what you have learned'. 'Understood'. 'Revealed about yourself'. Even as he thought those thoughts, he went back to that man Bukowski. That genius was way ahead of him – but at least he believed he was on that same path.

so you want to be a writer?

if it doesn't come bursting out of you
in spite of everything,
don't do it.
unless it comes unasked out of your
heart and your mind and your mouth
and your gut,
don't do it.
if you have to sit for hours
staring at your computer screen
or hunched over your
typewriter
searching for words,
don't do it.
if you're doing it for money or
fame,
don't do it.

if you're doing it because you want
women in your bed,
don't do it.
if you have to sit there and
rewrite it again and again,
don't do it.
if it's hard work just thinking about doing it,
don't do it.
if you're trying to write like somebody
else,
forget about it.
if you have to wait for it to roar out of
you,
then wait patiently.
if it never does roar out of you,
do something else.

if you first have to read it to your wife
or your girlfriend or your boyfriend
or your parents or to anybody at all,
you're not ready.

don't be like so many writers,
don't be like so many thousands of
people who call themselves writers,
don't be dull and boring and
pretentious, don't be consumed with self-
love.
the libraries of the world have
yawned themselves to
sleep
over your kind.
don't add to that.

don't do it.
unless it comes out of
your soul like a rocket,
unless being still would
drive you to madness or
suicide or murder,
don't do it.
unless the sun inside you is
burning your gut,
don't do it.

when it is truly time,
and if you have been chosen,
it will do it by
itself and it will keep on doing it
until you die or it dies in you.

there is no other way.

and there never was.

Charles Bukowski

One particular line jumped out at him, 'until you die or it dies in you'. He was beginning to feel it die. He had *seen* it die in him. Through the mirror. The lack of light behind his eyes. That's what it was. The words were fading, and nothing was filling the void that the process was creating. Not his understanding of spirituality. Not his drinking. Nothing. He felt death. Something inside him was dying and he was now convinced that it was his words. He had nothing else to say. The closer you feel connected with the divine – the less there *is* to say. He thought about that for a second. Every single word had been piled into a heap. A predetermined amount of words. It had taken him so long to build the fire, that he had forgotten just what was under the fuel of his words.

He gathered the Journals together. He wasn't organised enough to put them into years of continuity. Afterall, during some years, there was little, if any, writing done. Each and every one was taken from the drawer and placed into his Rucksack. He took a final look at how they sat before sealing the bag tight. 1984 was not among them. He still possessed that single thread of sentiment.

He went to the back door. Took the penultimate cigarette from its packet, whispering, 'The Son' before he lit it. He took an extra-long drag and savoured the nicotine. He noticed that the two starlings had disappeared. The sun was bright and bringing out the detail within the trees. The trees knew – but today they were saying nothing.

As he walked along the Canal, he was disappointed that the Swans were not in their usual place on the waterway. He couldn't see them anywhere. No Ducks. No Heron. No Canal boats. Just the poker-straight forge of silver water that tapered to a point in the distance. The only familiar element was the stillness.

He turned into the gap and made his way along the pathway that led him toward what was quickly becoming his favourite wood. He hadn't realised the first time he walked along it just how high the path went. It elevated him to a point from where he could see the knuckles of faraway hills in the west Pennines, but he didn't dwell on the view. He continued toward the wood. His wood.

His stomach felt empty. Not surprising as he had not been eating. The Journals were enough to carry. They were the contents of a full stomach. The trees had now lost all their leaves. They were not ashamed of their nakedness. The fabric of their branches now lay upon the ground. A carpet of golds, gilts and browns.

There was a clearing between two trees that afforded a view toward the town in the distance. With concentration and a squint,

it was possible to make out several landmarks. A church steeple. The tiny steel bones of a football stadium. He checked his wristwatch. 10:55am

He removed the Journals from his Rucksack one-by-one. He handled them with a reverence. Like you would a Hotel's Gideon bible. Not concerning yourself with what's inside. Just the fact that it is what it *is*. That's where the reverence comes from. The innate sense of knowing.

When he was satisfied that the books were piled in such a way – a skill he had learned from his time spent isolated on Scotland's 'Mull of Kintyre' as part of a training exercise – he pulled a cigarette lighter from his pocket – together with the packet of cigarettes that contained his final cigarette. 'The Holy Spirit'.

He thumbed for the date '20th September 1984'. 31 years to the day before his father had passed away. Ironically, it was one of the few days where he had said very little. Acknowledge simply with 'Stevie Wonder is still Number 1 with – I just called to say I love you. Crock of Shit'.

He lit the page with the flame from his cigarette lighter before the leaves fanned open as he turned the Journal upside down. Within seconds, the dry days of its paper each caught the fire and it was alight instantly. He used this as the seat for the other Journals and within a few minutes he was satisfied that they were all burning. The words of a life being eaten by fire. He checked his wristwatch again. It was 11:11am.

He sparked the cigarette from the fire's flames. He'd always been dramatic. Inhaled on the third and final cigarette in the trinity, 'The Holy Spirit', and enjoyed the hit.

He reflected on what could have been. There was probably enough in those Journals to inspire a book. There was enough emotion within the ink of their words to keep the fire burning for some time. He had spoken about school. His younger days. Adolescence. Relationships. Children. Girlfriends. Enemies. Friends. Family. Everything. It was all in there. He felt an element of sadness, but also a sense of relief. He wasn't that person anymore. He wasn't those people anymore. He needed to focus on what he was now. He was a much better person. He didn't need to dwell upon what had gone on in the past. He just needed to understand that it had shaped him. Let his demons' burn too – they're no use to him now and they know that too. They have no power over him. They've accepted their fate – like we all must accept that of our own. Know yourself. Accept yourself. Become the Creator.

The fire was producing heat now. He felt warm. At peace. He was glowing. Inside and out. There goes 1994. 1999. The years were all burning. All dying off. Transcending into the ether.

He looked up at the trees and could see black petals of burnt paper rising from the heat. Some appeared to skilfully pass between the thin branches of the tree-tops, before being blown on the faint wind in the direction of a favourite town.

For all the emotion written into the paper, each Journal was bone dry and they had burned quickly into a collective pile of black ash. The oneness of what the years had become made him smile. And he had convinced himself he rarely smiled. He threw the butt of his final cigarette onto the pile of ash. He smelt his sleeve and was surprised that he couldn't smell the effects of the fire's smoke. He reminded himself that his sense of 'smell' had never been his strongest point.

Satisfied that the Journals were spent – he gently used his foot to brush some of the brown and gilt leaves over the smoking seat of a fire. He walked back through the wood. Another reality beckoned.

31

The room had changed again. It felt less familiar. More clinical than he had ever remembered. He sat down. Stared directly toward the Interviewer. The Counsellor. The Enemy. It was midday. Precisely.

'How you feeling?'

'Brand new'.

'Really?'

'Yeah, absolutely'.

'Good. That's good news, really good news'. There was a slight pause.

'I've read your poetry-'

'And-?'

'Well, some of it is *very* surreal - and some of it is poignant-'

'You mean that the bits that should be surreal are poignant and the bits that are poignant are surreal - '

'Of course not. It's all very interesting -'

'I suppose that's one word for it – anyway, there won't be any more. I've stopped writing. No more Journal. No more poetry. Nothing. Time to 'do' and not to 'say.''

'Do you really believe that?'

'Why not? I've gone as far as I can go with it. The days when it once fell out of me are long gone. I haven't got the energy to sit there and feel it bleed from me. And I only write in those two ways. When it falls – and when it bleeds.'

'Isn't that how all good writers' write?'

'I never said I was a good writer. I just write.'

'So why have you decided to stop?'

'Because now feels like the time *to* stop.'

'Maybe, if you're feeling that if this is the time to stop – that's actually the best time to begin!'

Who is this guy?

'You know – Alpha/Omega. Nothing really begins or ends – it simply changes vibration. Goes up an octave – as it were. You convincing yourself that you're going to stop, sounds to me like being the ideal time to start writing again - '

'It's too late – I've burned all my Journals. Earlier – before I saw you'.

'Really?'

'Really.'

He handed me his pen. The fancy expensive one. The world's most dangerous pen. I can't remember what I'd called it. I didn't need to remember now anyway. What he'd called it. What we'd called it. Does it really matter?

'I want you to shut your eyes for a few seconds and think of a phrase. It can be as many words as you want – but as long as it makes sense to both you - and to anyone else who may read it.'

Him and his games. This guy's crazy.

'Ok.' He handed me a piece of paper with his right hand - and I took it with my left. After which, he produced what looked like my poetry and papers from a bag.

'Close your eyes. Have a think. There's no rush...'

The room was silent. No ticking clock. No pipes expanding. Silence. I kept my eyes closed and waited for a phrase to appear from out of the dark. It was dark. Total darkness. I had been here before. Many times. I knew what this was. I kept my eyes closed and as a phrase grew in my mind's eye – I quickly scribbled it down on the paper without opening my eyes. Why do I do this?

The space was getting warmer. Still no command from the Interviewer. No instruction. I didn't want to open my eyes. I was torn between the comfort of the dark or the reality. I wasn't sure what either one of those two things meant. Some days they felt the same. I think today is going to be one of those days. I'm going to count to 3 – then open my eyes. I know how I love my trilogies.

One. Why is he not talking to me?

Two. Oh god, oh god…

Three.

I opened my eyes and saw what I knew I'd see. Myself. Looking back at me through the reflection of a mirror. My bathroom mirror. My insanity was complete.

I leaned forward to look at myself. Whoever I was? I saw my eyes. The deadness behind them. Now that the words had gone too. I had nothing left. I destroy everything that I love and everything that wants to love me. My family. My loves. My words. The only thing that fills my eyes now is the insane madness. The overwhelming sense of realisation was pricked by what I had written on the piece of paper. I couldn't look. There were too many illusions to comprehend. Too many to begin to start understanding. It was too much. Much, much too much.

Yet another voice came from the ether. It sounded like my father's. The first time I'd hear his voice since he passed. 'Look…LOOK!' It was his voice.

I picked the piece of paper up and tilted my left hand. I had only written two words. I could only just make them both out from the scribble.

'Don't try'.

I knew exactly what that meant, and so too did my equally comforting madness.

He smiled – and he rarely smiled - at his reflection. And the insanity smiled right back.

Part V

32

There was a fine gap separating the curtains. It was morning. At least that's what the light was indicating.

He awoke naturally, and today he was being encouraged to wake quickly by the pattern of bright sunshine that was sitting on a bedroom wall, refracted through a glass vase. He had no idea what was the time? It felt around 10 am.

He instinctively looked through his bedroom window. As much to gauge the weather and as much to have a nosey. His bedroom faced a car park, where the other flats' occupants parked their vehicles. There were 2 cars in their spaces. It was well after 9am.

He saw two cats. A black cat. A tortoise shell cat. The tortoise shell feline was following the black cat as they carefully negotiated the fine beam of a fence top. It seemed unusual to see two cats doing that at the same time. In another life he would have imagined it was a glitch in the Matrix. He paused for a second. Some things never leave you.

It looked like a beautiful, sunny day. It was always pot -luck on the first day of spring. 'The last day of winter can be warmer than the first day of spring' – popped into his head. It looked like a lovely day – so he was going to take advantage of it.

Once up and dressed, he inhaled on his Vape cigarette. It wasn't as satisfying as a real cigarette, but he had finally succumbed to the poverty in which he was living. There were people a lot worse off than him. He really did understand that. With the money that he was trying to save from not smoking, he was going to go wandering. That's *who* he had decided he was.

That's *what* he had decided he was. A wanderer. The more he understood it – the more at peace he became. A once troubled soul – a bit like David Banner – mooching about – to the outsider, 'mooching with no real purpose' - to those who understand, 'just doing what it is they do – them wandering types'. He'd accepted that. It was a great way to avoid being 'sad' or 'lonely'.

He hadn't written anything since the day he burned his Journals. Since the day he was last ill. He wasn't even sure if he was ill? Some people say so – others just let him get on with it. It's not a disease. You can't see it. You rarely see its manifestations. The moments of acute 'madness'. 'Visions'. 'Conversations'. 'Hallucinations'. It's not all bad. Madness is a great guest at creativity parties. He'd stopped fighting it. It was only on the very few occasions it turned up unannounced. Often, it's not uninvited. It's encouraged sometimes. Not today. Today is going to be peaceful.

It was unseasonably warm. It was officially winter only the day before, and today along the canal, it felt like early summer. Global warming activists would be frothing at the gills.

He had started to take a different route along the waterway. Instead of walking along the straight and narrow path – he'd turned left at the bridge and followed the walkway that bends quickly out of sight. You never know what's ahead that way. Always the maverick. He was absorbing the colours as he walked. The light – detailing the fineness in everything. It really was a beautiful day.

The word 'Serafina' popped into his head. Literally from nowhere. Serafina? He rummaged through a pile of thoughts quickly and realised that it was the name he had given to a hotel receptionist in one of his Journal entries. His attempt at dumping erotica on a page under the guise of some convoluted fantasy tale. He liked the name. Ser-a-fina. He quickly remembered the tale. He wondered what ever happened to her. He realised that he had created her. That *anything* could happen. Anything that *he* decided. If he was still writing. Become the Creator. He wasn't. It'd left him.

He walked along a few more paces, before he heard the trees and the bushes rustling in a few gusts of wind. Everything was about to renew itself. Spring is a favourite time of the year. The renaissance of nature. Another old mantra popped into his mind. Know yourself. Accept yourself. Become the Creator. Until you die – or it dies in you. And there he felt it. He looked at the trees and the trees, those beautiful trees, simply loved him back. He smiled to himself – he would now always smile when he felt it. Now that he had it. The strength that only weakness allows.